BOARD OF EDUCATION
DISTRICT 150
SOUTH HOLLAND, ILLINOIS

LITTLE RED

LITTLE RED

By

Roberta Piper

Illustrated by *Joan Berg*

CHARLES SCRIBNER'S SONS,　New York

For *Andy*
    Jonathan

    Anne
    Mark

CONTENTS

LITTLE RED

I

One Hundred and Ten

"Ouch," said Nan Coburn to her mother. "You pulled."

Mrs. Coburn kept on with slow steady strokes of the brush. "Rats' nests," she said. Nan smiled, because that was their special joke, that rats made nests in her hair at night and caused all the snarls. All the same, she wished her hair was short like Jean's. Then she could comb it herself, and there wouldn't be any snarls and she wouldn't have to stand still.

"I wish it was all cut off," Nan said.

"Such pretty hair. It would be a shame to cut it."

Mrs. Coburn was braiding now, and Nan could feel the braid pulling tight and her mother's fingers working in and out with the three smooth strands. When the braids were finished, she liked the way they felt—clean

and stiff. And she liked the way they thumped on her back when she ran, a half a thump behind her feet, as though her braids could not quite keep up with her. But she did not like standing still while the braids were made. She poked the things on the bathroom shelf—old buttons and shell hairpins and a penny and a silver buttonhook which was always on that shelf, although no one ever used it except to fish for things that got lost in the drain. Mrs. Coburn began on the second braid and Nan shook her head to be sure the first braid felt right.

"Do stop fidgeting," Mrs. Coburn said.

Nan sighed. Every morning it seemed to take so long to do her hair.

"Could I have this penny?" she asked, fingering it.

Mrs. Coburn looked up. "I guess so."

Nan slipped the penny in her pocket while her mother twisted the rubber band on the end of the braid.

"I don't want bows," Nan said when Mrs. Coburn reached for the ribbons on the shelf.

"Oh, Nan," Mrs. Coburn said. "The other girls. . ."

But Nan slipped out of the bathroom and hurried along to the kitchen where her father and grandfather were already sitting down to breakfast.

"Well, hi, Old Top," her father greeted her.

"I don't know why she's so set against bows," Mrs. Coburn said, as she followed her into the room with the ribbons still in her hands.

"They slow her down probably," Mr. Coburn said, and Nan was pleased by his comment. That wasn't why she didn't want ribbons. She didn't even know why she didn't want ribbons. But somehow, underneath the joking, her father understood.

There were so many things she wanted and so many things she didn't want, and most of the time, when her mother asked her why, why, she felt mixed up and she didn't know why. She wanted a pony. She knew just the pony she wanted at Reed's pony farm and she wanted it just because it was there, alive and warm and brown and not big like Molly and Gyp. And she wanted a whole dollar of her own to spend at the Fair next week— not a quarter now and a dime later and another quarter after lunch—but a dollar all at once, her own to spend so that she could ride on the ponies whenever she liked. Most of all she wanted a pony, and her grandfather had said that maybe when she was old enough he'd get her a pony. But she never seemed to be old enough. She thought she'd ask about the dollar again. She finished her oatmeal and milk in a hurry so that she'd have time to ask before she had to go to school.

"Fair *is* next week," she said and waited.

"Hmph," said her grandfather with a twinkle in his eye. "I thought you'd forgotten that."

"Could I have a—a dollar of my own—for the Fair?" she blurted.

Mr. Coburn grinned at her, but he didn't say anything and neither did her grandfather.

"Couldn't I? Please?"

Her grandfather pushed his chair away from the table and leaned back, balancing on two legs, twiddling his thumbs around each other, first one way and then the other, which was a game he played with himself.

"How's your arithmetic coming?" he asked. "Do you think you could keep track of a dollar? Adding and subtracting doesn't seem to be your strong point, does it?"

"I—I think I could," Nan said. "I got a hundred a lot of times—well, I got a hundred once last week. It was adding and subtracting both. Big addition, too."

"I guess I might give you a dollar, if you did something extra good in arithmetic," her grandfather said.

"Oh, Grandpa," Nan breathed.

"Say, for instance, if you got a hundred and ten on a paper someday between now and Fair time."

"But Grandpa! You can't get a hundred and ten." Nan cried. "A hundred is when you get them all right. You can't get any more than that."

"You always ought to be able to do better than all right," her grandfather said. "A good horse trader in this world can always figure some way to do better than all right. Got to figure a little this way and a little that way, give the other fellow something he wants and he'll be more than likely to give you what you want."

"But this isn't horses. It's arithmetic!" she said. "You're teasing. You must be teasing."

"Nope, I'm not teasing. I made you an offer—a dollar if you get a hundred and ten in arithmetic, all fair and square."

"It's time for you to get off to school or you won't get there in time for arithmetic," Mrs. Coburn said.

While she was putting on her sweater in the hall, she heard her mother say, "Well, that ought to take her mind off getting her hair cut for a few days anyway."

So they were teasing her—even her mother, joking about her hair. She went out and let the screen door bang hard. None of them thought she could do it. And she didn't see how she could do it either. A hundred and ten. Nobody ever got a hundred and ten—and she didn't even get a hundred very often. It would have been hard enough if her grandfather had said a dollar if she got a hundred. But he wouldn't change now, she knew that. And he'd give the money to her if she did get a hundred and ten. He always kept his word.

That morning Nan had trouble keeping her mind on her work, even in reading, which she liked. In arithmetic, the numbers looked like crazy squiggles she had never seen before, and when the teacher marked her paper, the answers were almost half wrong. She got a red fifty at the top of the page, the worst she had ever done.

Then she did the first bit of adding she had done that day that made any sense. Fifty and sixty made a hundred and ten. Maybe if she got just sixty tomorrow, Miss Dunbar would let her add the two marks together. Nan laughed out loud at the idea of getting over a hundred when she had made more mistakes than usual.

"Nan!" said Miss Dunbar from across the room.

Nan quickly looked down at her geography book. And then she began to think about Miss Dunbar. Miss Dunbar kept you working. She didn't let you giggle the way Mrs. Foote, last year, had done. Sometimes, even Mrs. Foote had giggled too and said silly things. She could have asked Mrs. Foote to play a joke on her grandfather and mark a paper a hundred and ten. But not Miss Dunbar. She wasn't often cross and sometimes they had fun, but she didn't let you get away with things. Nan looked at Miss Dunbar who was leaning against the wall, her arms folded, her eyes squinted against the sun.

"Nan," Miss Dunbar said warningly, "get to work now."

It was no use. She could never ask her. There was just no way she could get an arithmetic paper marked a hundred and ten.

After supper that night, when everyone was sitting around the library table in the living room, Nan thought about it some more. The more she thought about it, the more unhappy she felt. Her mother was writing in her diary. Every night she did that.

"Let's see," Mrs. Coburn asked, "how many cans of corn did I figure it made altogether with the ten I did today? Was it ninety-five, or did I say it was ninety-eight?" Mrs. Coburn always kept a record of the canning she did, so that she would know how many cans of vegetables and fruit they used each winter.

"Well, I don't seem to remember now what you did say," Mr. Coburn answered. "I guess you'll have to count them again."

"Get Nan here to count them for you," her grandfather said. "She's practicing arithmetic. It will do her good."

"That's so," said her mother. "But she probably has her mind so set on one number by now that if she counts them, they'll come out a hundred and ten."

Nan smiled in spite of herself. "I guess that's the only thing that will be a hundred and ten then," she said.

"Ho, you haven't given up so soon, have you?" her grandfather asked.

"Yes, but Grandpa," Nan burst out, "you don't know Miss Dunbar. She—well, she thinks arithmetic is—is—serious. She wouldn't think it was fair to give me a hundred and ten."

"No, of course not. I wouldn't think it was fair to

give you a hundred and ten either. The thing is—the way
I told you this morning—you've got to make a trade.
You figure what she wants, and give it to her, and then
you get what you want. Make her a proposition and see
what she says. You say, I'll do this for you, if you do
something else for me."

"You mean like staying after school to erase the boards
for her?" Nan asked.

"Well, now, that doesn't seem to me to have much to
do with arithmetic. It seems to me it ought to be more of
something right there on the arithmetic paper."

"But, Grandpa, you can't do any more if you've
got them all right—or do you mean do some extra
problems?"

"Now you're thinking. That's more like it. Just see
what she says if you go at it like that."

In the morning Nan forgot to fuss about her hair, even
when her mother pulled. She didn't even notice that her
mother put on blue hair ribbons to match her dress.
She was thinking, thinking, thinking. She was thinking
when she could talk to Miss Dunbar, and just what
she'd say. If she hurried with her breakfast, she might
get to school in time to talk to Miss Dunbar before the
bell rang.

When Nan went into the school room, Miss Dunbar
was drawing a map of North America on the board.

She was working carefully with colored chalk, and Nan did not want to disturb her, so she walked slowly to the blackboard a few feet away from Miss Dunbar and began making designs in the chalk dust with an eraser. Perhaps Miss Dunbar would say something and then she could ask her. Very soon the other children would come in, and the bell would ring, and then there would be no chance to talk.

At last Miss Dunbar said, "Hello, Nan." But she was still looking at the board, squinting a little, behind her glasses. Then suddenly Nan had an idea. There was something—something special—that Miss Dunbar had been asking her to do all year on her papers. Now she thought she knew why. Miss Dunbar squinted when she looked at things. Nan remembered she had once heard her mother say that Miss Dunbar had trouble with her eyes. And that was one reason why Miss Dunbar had asked her to make her papers neater. Just then Miss Dunbar turned around.

"Well, Nan," Miss Dunbar said, "has something been bothering you?"

"Yes, Miss Dunbar." Now the moment had come, but even with all her thinking, Nan did not know what to say. It was hard to know where to begin. "Yes—you see—not bothering, exactly, but—I—it's my grand-father—or—well, it's arithmetic really."

"You don't need to worry about that," Miss Dunbar said. "Most of the time now your arithmetic is much better."

"But I—if I got everything right and made the numbers especially neat, would you give me a hundred and ten instead of just a hundred? A hundred for its being all right and ten for neatness?"

Nan felt herself blushing. She had thought she could not tell Miss Dunbar why she wanted a hundred and ten, but now she had to. "Because my grandfather said. . ." she began. "You see, I wanted a dollar of my own to spend at the Fair, and my grandfather said if I got a hundred and ten in arithmetic, he'd give it to me. He said if I did something extra—like some extra problems— maybe you'd give me a hundred and ten. Only I thought, well, you're always saying I should be neater, so I thought. . ."

Miss Dunbar threw back her head and laughed. Then she said, "Neatness would be something extra for you, wouldn't it?" She was still smiling and Nan smiled too. She waited. Miss Dunbar was still looking at her. "Yes," she said at last, "I think neatness would be worth ten."

"Oh, thank you," said Nan. And she twirled around and hurried out the door and through the hall onto the playground and then she ran and ran and ran, with her braids thumping across her back with each step.

In arithmetic that day Nan worked very carefully. She copied the problems in full round figures and set the answers exactly under the line. She wished arithmetic wasn't so hard. If it were just made up of words like spelling, instead of numbers, Nan knew she wouldn't have any trouble. She could get a hundred in spelling any day. And there were some people who could do that in arithmetic. There was Rebecca Snow, the smallest girl in the class, who sat one seat in front of Nan and one row over. She almost never said anything, even on the playground, and she never raised her hand. But when Miss Dunbar called on her in arithmetic, she always knew the answer right off, no matter how hard the problem was. Nan sighed. She wished she could do arithmetic like that. But she couldn't. Instead she added each set of figures a second time.

When she had finished, she was almost sure that she hadn't made a mistake, and the paper didn't look at all like her usual hurried scrawl where the numbers ran into each other and the answers tumbled away from the problems.

She watched Miss Dunbar grading the papers. Her grandfather would laugh when she told him and showed him the paper. At last Miss Dunbar called her to the desk. As she walked up the aisle, Miss Dunbar shook her head ever so slightly. She was telling her, then, that there had been a mistake. Nan looked at her neat lovely paper in dismay. At the top in red crayon was written *96—Very Neat*, and near the end there was a red check next to a problem.

$$\begin{array}{r} 293 \\ 161 \\ \hline 354 \end{array}$$

"Do you see what's wrong?" asked Miss Dunbar.

Nan looked at the paper and then nodded. "I forgot to carry the one."

"Don't worry," Miss Dunbar said. "There are four more arithmetic lessons before Fair Day. And it was *very* neat."

That was Wednesday. On Thursday and Friday, Nan's papers were neat, but there were two mistakes on Thursday and one on Friday. At home, Nan refused to talk about arithmetic, or what Miss Dunbar had said. On Saturday, there was no chance even to try to get a hundred and ten. She went in the kitchen and found her mother packing the best jars of jams and jellies and canned fruits and vegetables in boxes, ready to go to the Fair on Wednesday. Usually, Nan liked to look at the jars—the bright red of strawberries, flecked with yellow seeds, the deep rich red of raspberry jam, the green beans packed upright and the yellow mush of corn that she had helped scrape from the cob. Today it only reminded her that Fair Day was almost here. In the barn it was no better. Her grandfather was brushing the shiny coat of his favorite registered Shorthorn cow.

From the barn window, she saw her father out in the field, digging the last of the turnips. She ran out across the stubble and began carrying turnips to the wagon. Her father kept on digging until he had finished the field and then, together, they loaded the turnips and climbed up onto the wagon.

"Guess that about does it for this year," her father said with satisfaction. "The corn is in, potatoes are in, and now the turnips. It can freeze as hard as it wants to now, I don't care. I'll be ready for a day off at the Fair by Wednesday."

"Oh, the Fair!" Nan groaned.

"What's the matter, Old Top? Are you still worrying over that arithmetic? I thought you and Miss Dunbar would have that all worked out by now. She's an old friend of your Grandpa's, you know."

"She is?" Nan asked.

"Sure. Her father and your grandfather have been swapping horses for sixty or seventy years now. Guess she'd go along with any scheme she thought would get a dollar out of your Grandpa. That's one reason he put you up to it."

Nan laughed. That explained why Miss Dunbar had been so amused. But then Nan looked sober again. "We've got it fixed all right. It's not her, it's me." Then she told her father about the three days when she had been extra neat and had tried to be extra careful and how each time there had been at least one mistake.

Her father nodded. "Yep. I expect you're trying too hard."

"Trying *too* hard?" Nan exclaimed.

"Here, I'll show you what I mean. You see that fence post, there." Mr. Coburn pulled up the horses and stopped the wagon. "Suppose I want to hit that fence post, second one down from the corner. And I need to hit it right now, first shot." He picked up a turnip, aimed carefully, snapped his wrist back and threw the turnip. It struck the ground beyond the fence post and rolled on down the hill. The horses moved restlessly and Mr. Coburn said, "Whoa, there." Then he looked at Nan and said, "Now suppose I just kind of want to hit that post for fun." He pulled his arm back lazily and the turnip spun through the air and thumped against the fence post. "I learned that, pitching for the town base-ball team. If you try too hard to put a strike across, you're likely to end up hitting the batter. I guess you might do the same thing adding too. You try too hard, and you make a mistake."

On Monday Nan began her arithmetic slowly, re-
membering the turnips and what her father had said.
Today she was just going to do a good job, she wasn't
going to try too hard. Suddenly the numbers seemed
almost to be adding themselves; she remembered the
carry-ones and the carry-twos and everything came out
right. She was sure this time. Then, when it was almost
time to pass her paper in, she looked at it in sudden
horror—she had forgotten about being neat. Quickly
she got another paper and began neatly copying the
problems and answers. Then she thought, I must still
relax, or I'll make a mistake copying. Relax and hurry.
Hurry. Relax. But already it was time for arithmetic
class to be over. She looked at the clock and then she
looked at Miss Dunbar. She found that Miss Dunbar was
looking at her, and Miss Dunbar smiled. Then Nan
realized that Miss Dunbar was giving her time to finish.
She could relax now, there was no need to hurry. Then
at last she was through. She sat up straight and folded
her hands on her desk until Miss Dunbar looked up and
asked her to collect the papers.

When school was over that·afternoon, Nan stayed
behind for a minute to say thank you to Miss Dunbar.
She had in her hand the arithmetic paper which said in
red crayon across the top:

$$\begin{array}{r} 100 \\ \text{Neatness} \quad \underline{10} \\ 110 \end{array}$$

Miss Dunbar looked at the paper and smiled. "Tell your grandfather," she said, "I may be able to teach you arithmetic, but he's certainly the one who is going to teach you to be a good horse trader."

2

Little Red

The following Wednesday, the morning of the Fair, Nan got out of bed and dressed while it was still dark. She could hear the scrape and clatter of pots and pans from the kitchen, and outside, in the dim light, she could see the brown shapes of the cows pushing through the barnyard into the field. There was a clang of milk pails and the chatter of voices when her father and grandfather came in from the morning chores. Nan hurried with the buttons on her dress and took her shoes to the kitchen to put on, so that she wouldn't miss anything.

"Is it going to be a good day?" she asked. "It won't rain, will it?"

Out of the kitchen window, she could see mist swirling over the barn roof, and the grass in the fields was silvered with frost.

"There's a lot of fog along the river," her father said. "But it will burn off as soon as the sun's up."

When they had finished breakfast, her grandfather pulled his leather pouch from his pocket and dumped some money out into his hand. Out of the handful of change, he picked a half dollar and two quarters, and gave them to Nan.

"How much does that make?" he asked.

"A dollar," she said.

"Now you've got all that money, what are you going to do with it?" her mother inquired.

Nan didn't need to think about that. She had known from the beginning what she would do if she got a dollar.

"Ride on the ponies," she said. "I can ride ten times for a dollar."

"Are you going to spend a dollar riding on ponies?" her father asked. "You can ride on Gyp and Molly for nothing, any day, right here at home."

"But they're not ponies," she said. "They're big, clumpy, old workhorses."

"Let her be," her grandfather said. "She got her hundred and ten in arithmetic, and now she's got her dollar, all fair and square. Let her spend it the way she wants."

It seemed hours to Nan, waiting while her father and grandfather went off to get cleaned up, and her mother packed sandwiches and pies and doughnuts for their

lunch. She helped put the hardboiled eggs in a box, and
then she peeked into the box that held the pies to see if
she could tell what kind they were. She took her money
out of her pocket and laid it out on the pantry shelf and
made it into a pile with the half dollar at the bottom and
the quarters neatly stacked on top. Mrs. Coburn hurried
in and out of the pantry, putting coffee in a thermos, and
fresh water in a jar.

"Nan, do get out from underfoot," her mother said.
"And get your sweater. And get that little brown purse
to put your money in, before you lose it. Too much
money for her to be carrying around anyway," she
added, under her breath, as though Nan wasn't right
there, listening.

Suddenly Nan was unhappy. Her mother didn't
want her to have a dollar all her own. The money felt
heavy and strange in her pocket. Maybe she ought to
let her mother keep it for her. Maybe she would lose
it if she kept it herself. Then she thought of the warm
brown neck of her favorite pony, and how soft it would
feel when she put her cheek against it, and she remembered the smooth leathery shine of the saddle. She
slipped her hand into her pocket and touched the money.
She knew now what she would do. As soon as they got to
the Fair, she would give all the money to Mr. Reed, and
then she wouldn't lose it, and she could go back for her
pony rides anytime.

At last they were all ready. Mrs. Coburn had gone back once to see that the fire in the kitchen was out, and then she had gone back again to get the picnic blanket. Nan sat in the back of the car next to her grandfather. She didn't like the smell of her grandfather's cigar, and when they started, the gentle swing of the car made her stomach feel funny. Sometimes when they were out riding, she felt so sick that they had to stop the car. But she couldn't do that today. If she did, her mother would make her get out and sit on the grass near the car before they went on again. And when they got to the Fair, she might not be allowed to ride on the ponies at all. So she clenched her teeth and told herself she must not be sick.

On the main road there were dozens of cars, all headed for the Fair. The Connor family went by, with the boys huddled under a blanket in the back of the truck. Bob waved at Nan and shouted something she couldn't hear. Once at school, Bob had told Nan that his father was going to get him a pony—maybe a real Indian pony, someday. Nan wished that she could have an Indian pony. She wished, too, that she could ride in the back of a truck, with the wind blowing her hair, and no cigar smoke. Then she just wished they would hurry up and get there.

Near the fairground, the line of cars slowed down, stopping and starting, edging nearer the gate. She could hear a band playing far off, and the sound of many voices, and the mooing of cows in the cattle sheds. When she stood up and leaned over the front seat of the car between her father and mother, she could see the tops of the tents below her and the ferris wheel and the grand-stand with flags flying, and the smooth brown loop of the race track. For one moment, it was so exciting, Nan was sure she was going to be sick. And then, on a little hill, right where it had been last year, she saw Reed's pony truck and beside it, the little ring and the ponies tied in a row. It was all right; they were there. Her grandfather's cigar had gone out, and she knew she wasn't going to be sick now.

When they had crossed the track and parked on the grass meadow which was already lined with cars, Nan jumped out and started off in the direction of the ponies.

"Nan!" her mother said, reprovingly.

"You're in kind of a hurry, aren't you?" her father asked. "You can't run off by yourself like that."

"Nobody will know where you are," her mother added. "I thought we'd go and see the exhibits first, and look at the animals."

"Plenty of time for your rides after that," her father said. "You can't be riding all day, not even with a whole dollar."

Nan's heart sank. Didn't they know how much she

wanted to see the ponies? The exhibits and the animals would take all morning. And then there would be horse pulling and vaudeville on the stage, and then it would be time for lunch and the sulky races would start. She wouldn't get to see the ponies until ever so late.

"I could go to the ponies by myself," Nan said. "And then I'd just stay there. I wouldn't get lost."

"Now, Nan . . . ." her mother began.

Her grandfather interrupted. "I've got to talk to a man about some business. How would it be if Nan went along with me? Unless she'd rather see the jams and jellies, of course."

"Oh, no," Nan said. "Mom, could I go with Grandpa —couldn't I, please?"

Her mother laughed. "All right," she said. "But one of you two remember to come back when it's noon, or you won't get anything to eat. Of course they'll go straight off to the ponies," she added.

Together, Nan and her grandfather walked back across the track and up the hill toward the ponies. Twice her grandfather stopped to talk to men he knew. And once he hooked the crook of his cane around the leg of a man who was talking to someone else, and Nan was afraid the man would be angry. But he turned around and clapped her grandfather on the shoulder and said, "Well, if it isn't Charlie, up to his old tricks." And her grandfather said, "Simon, you old timer, how's the world treating you?" Then Nan knew they were teasing each other, just like the boys did at school.

When they went past the merry-go-round with its music playing and the ferris wheel with its different colored seats, Nan wished she could ride on them, too. But she wanted to save all her money for the ponies.

At last they reached the top of the little hill, and her grandfather sat down on the tail gate of the pony truck, out of breath, and motioned with his cane for Nan to go along and ride. Nan looked for the brown pony, her favorite, and at first she couldn't see him. Perhaps they'd left him at the farm, she thought. They had dozens of ponies on the farm, and only eight or ten of them came to the Fair. There were five ponies with saddles on, hitched at the rail, ready for the rides, and none of these was the one she liked. Then she saw more ponies, staked out in the grass beyond the ring, and there, near the front of the truck was the one she had been looking for.

She took a piece of apple that she had brought in her pocket and held it out on the flat of her hand and walked slowly toward the pony, talking in a low voice so that the pony would know she was coming and wouldn't be frightened.

"Hi, boy, hey, there. Easy, boy," she said.

The pony lifted his head and stared at Nan. Slowly Nan moved closer and held the apple out. The pony

reached his head as far as the rope would let him, and tipping his head to one side, he curled his soft black lip over the apple and took it in his teeth. She ran her hand along the pony's neck, and the pony shivered his muscles as though he was trying to drive off a fly. Nan laughed. Next time she patted him firmly, and the pony stood still.

A boy came around the truck just then, carrying two pails full of water. "There are ponies over there, saddled up, if you want to ride," he said.

"Couldn't I ride this one?" Nan asked.

"What, Little Red, there?" he said. "He's just getting broken in to the ring, and he doesn't like it much. He's a touchy one. You'd better leave him alone. Besides, I haven't got time to saddle him up now. You'll have to ride one that's already saddled, if you want to ride."

Nan ran her hand along the pony's neck. The pony put his head down and nosed her shoes. She leaned over and curled her fingers in the pony's mane. Then the pony lifted his head so suddenly that his neck came up under her chin with a bang and made her bite her tongue. For a moment it hurt so that tears came to her eyes, and she stepped back and leaned against the truck. When she looked up she saw that the boy was watching her.

"I told you, you'd better look out for him," he said. "He bites sometimes, too."

"He didn't mean to do that," Nan said. "It was my fault, leaning over."

The boy shrugged his shoulders and picked up the water pails. "Okay, it's your chin."

When the boy had gone, she patted the pony again and held out another piece of apple. "Good Little Red," she said, and the pony took the apple as carefully as he had before.

Nan said good-bye to Little Red and went over to the ring. She stood in line, and when her turn came, she rode on a fat brown and white pony which walked slowly and carefully, twice around the ring, and then went back to its hitching place. Just as she was getting in line for another ride, Nan heard her grandfather calling. She went over to the truck where her grandfather was talking to Mr. Reed.

"So you're the girl that's going to have the pony, are you?" Mr. Reed asked, when Nan came up to them.

Nan couldn't believe it. "Really, Grandpa?" she asked. "Am I really going to have one? Right now?"

"Well, I thought this would be a good time to get one, while Mr. Reed's got them right here near home."

"Oh, Grandpa!" Nan exclaimed. "Thank you, oh, thank you."

"Now," Mr. Reed began, "the kind of pony you want is a three- or four-year-old—young enough to have a good lot of life in him yet, and old enough so he's trained and used to saddle and bridle and gotten rid of any bad tricks he might have. Take the spotted one there, Priscilla. She'd make a good little riding pony for the girl. Or Black Boy. He's a little hard in the mouth, but you use a double bit on him and he'll go along as nice as you please."

Grandfather got up and stepped over to the pony ring. He walked around the first pony, looking at its legs and running his hand along its back. Next he opened its mouth and looked at its teeth.

"Any one of them here in the ring would make you a good little pony," Mr. Reed said.

"This one is nearer eight years old than three, or I'll eat my hat," Grandfather said. "Don't try to sell me that for a three-year-old."

"Well, he's a little older than some of them," Mr. Reed agreed. "He's—let's see—about six, maybe seven years old."

"Grandpa," Nan plucked at his coat sleeve, "Grandpa, I like the one that's hitched in front of the truck. Do you think I could have him?"

"Little Red?" Mr. Reed said, looking surprised. "He's a two-year-old. He's going to be a nice pony in another year or two. Your girl's got a good eye for a horse. But he's a two-year-old. He isn't what I'd call fully broken, and he's got one or two bad tricks yet."

"I rode him when we were up at your farm this summer," Nan said. "And he's the one I like best."

"Yes, I guess we must have had him in working with him that day. Oh, he'd be all right with someone that could really manage him."

Nan's grandfather walked up to Little Red and looked him over as carefully as he had the others. He looked in his mouth and he lifted up each hoof and felt his legs. "At least you aren't far off on *his* age," he said. He and Mr. Reed eyed each other and grinned. Nan watched them and thought, Grandpa is horse-trading now, and it's fun for him.

"So you think she'd have trouble handling this horse?" Grandpa asked.

"She might. She might not," Mr. Reed shrugged.

"Well, let's put a saddle on him and see how she makes out."

Nan rode twice slowly around the ring on Little Red, and it was not at all like riding on the fat spotted pony. Under her, she could feel the ripple of Little Red's muscles, and she felt him tense up and skit sideways a bit when they went by the line of hitched ponies. Little Red didn't stop when they had been around twice.

Gently, Nan pressed her heels against his sides, and Little Red moved into an easy trot. Oh, I like him, Nan thought; I do hope I can have Little Red.

With his cane, her grandfather motioned her to stop, and she reined in and took Little Red up to the fence.

"Think you can handle him?" her grandfather asked. She nodded.

"That's the one you want, then?"

She nodded again. She was really going to have Little Red for her very own. She saw her grandfather talking to Mr. Reed again, so she got off Little Red and went over to listen, to be sure that there wasn't any mistake.

"Now if I take that pony," her grandfather was saying, "can you find an old saddle around here, and a bridle and a halter, that you can throw in, too? We'll have to have some gear to go along with the pony."

"I guess we can probably find something that will do," Mr. Reed agreed.

"And the girl will be wanting to ride some today," Grandfather said.

"She can ride all she wants, any pony she wants, free," Mr. Reed said.

"And now, I guess we'd better hustle along to the car or there won't be anything left to eat, Nan," said her grandfather.

When they were going down the hill, Nan danced

along beside her grandfather, scuffing up dust in the road, until he whacked her playfully with the cane. "Gosh all hemlock, but you're full of ginger," he said.

"A pony—a pony and all the rides I want today," Nan sang.

"And a saddle and a bridle and a halter," her grandfather added. "Don't you forget your Gramp's an old horse trader. And remember, first time that pony runs away with you, you were the one who wanted it."

When they reached the car and had told everything— or almost everything—about their morning with the ponies, and Nan had described three times exactly what Little Red looked like, and Grandfather had told how he got Mr. Reed to throw in a saddle and bridle and halter for the price of the pony, Nan's mother said, "I hope it's a good safe pony."

"Well, he's . . ." Nan began, but her grandfather interrupted.

"He's the safest two-year-old they've got up there," he said, and he winked at Nan because none of the others knew that Little Red was the only two-year-old pony that Mr. Reed had at the Fair.

When they had picked up the remains of the food and put the blanket back in the car, the whole family set out to see the new pony. On the way, Nan put her hand into her pocket and found the change from her dollar,

still there, even though she had forgotten about it.
Finding it there was a wonderful surprise. Now that she
could ride on the ponies as much as she wanted, free,
she could use the money to ride on the merry-go-round

and the ferris wheel and the swings. Then she thought
she would like some cotton candy and before she went
home, she would get a big yellow balloon. It was the
best Fair Day she could ever remember.

3

In the Mud

Nan sat on the porch railing, looking down the road. "Will they be here soon?" she asked.

Her grandfather reached out from his rocking chair and poked her gently in the ribs with his cane. "You're getting kind of impatient, aren't you?"

"The man said four o'clock, and it's already quarter past four," she reminded him. Ever since she got home from school, she had been impatient, first darting into the kitchen to look at the clock, and then racing out to the road, then back to her grandfather.

"They'll get here just as soon, if you stop fidgeting," Mrs. Coburn called from the kitchen.

"But I want them to come now," Nan said. "Pretty soon, it will be dark, and I won't be able to ride tonight."

Mrs. Coburn came to stand in the doorway. "Well then, there'll be tomorrow and the day after and the day after that," she said. "Patience doesn't seem to be one of your long suits, does it?"

"Oh, Mother . . ." Nan began to protest.

"Pst," her grandfather interrupted, holding up his hand for silence and cocking his head on one side. "Hear that?" he said. "That sounds like a truck coming over the bridge."

Nan hopped off the porch railing and raced down the path to the road. She heard the rumble of wheels and then the pony truck appeared around the curve and came slowly along the road. When it pulled into the yard, she could hear the restless patter of the ponies moving around, so that the truck itself seemed almost alive. By the time it stopped and Mr. Reed got out, her grandfather had come down from the porch and Mr. Coburn was hurrying along from the barn.

Nan skipped over to meet her father. "Can I ride him right now?" she asked, jumping up and down.

Her father smiled. "Let's get him unloaded first," he said.

"Where would be the best place to unload?" Mr. Reed asked.

"How about that bank under the lilac bushes?" Mr. Coburn said. "If you back up there and let down the ramp against the bank, it won't be so steep."

"That's fine." Mr. Reed got into the truck, turned it

around and backed up so that the double wheels on the back of the truck were at the bottom of the grassy bank. He got out and unhooked the heavy chains that held the back panel of the truck in place. Then he swung the panel down to make a ramp. There were cleats of wood nailed across the panel to give the ponies a foothold and the wood was worn and splintered.

As soon as the ramp was in place, Nan moved as close as she dared and looked into the truck. Little Red was hitched at the back, and beyond him, the ponies were packed in so tight that when one pony moved, all the others had to shift their positions too. There were pony legs, pony faces, pony ears, pony backs, in such confusion that it was hard to tell which head belonged with which tail. Nan laughed because it looked like a long lumpy shelf made of nothing but ponies.

Then Mr. Reed climbed into the truck and unhitched Little Red. Mr. Reed held the rope tight and started down the ramp, but Little Red braced his forefeet and stood still. When Mr. Reed pulled on the rope, Little Red arched his neck and stood firmly at the top of the ramp. His ears were laid back, his nostrils wide with fear, his eyes rolled so that they showed white.

"Oh, don't hurt him," Nan breathed.

"Don't worry. He'll be all right," her father assured her.

Mr. Reed shortened his hold on the rope and put one hand on Little Red's nose. "Easy there, boy," he said. "The darn pony has been down this ramp a dozen times and he's still got to get scared every time." He slipped his hand under the halter and leaned his weight against the rope. "Now!" he shouted. "Yip!"

Little Red's braced feet slid along the slippery wood, and then suddenly Mr. Reed lunged forward and Little Red scrambled after him down the ramp and onto the grass. For a moment, Little Red blew hard through his nostrils and then, as Mr. Reed loosened his hold on the rope, Little Red relaxed and put his head down to nibble some grass.

Mr. Reed stood with the end of the halter rope in his hand and the other hand on Little Red's shoulder. "Well, there's your pony," he said to Nan.

She walked up to the other side of Little Red and rested her hand on him, too, and smiled up at Mr. Reed. "Can I ride him now?" she asked.

"We'd better get him into the barn and let him settle down," her father said.

"I could just ride bareback, while you led him on the way to the barn."

"He looks skittish to me," her father said. "Better let the riding go until tomorrow."

"Being loaded in and out of the truck and bumping

around in there on the road doesn't help their disposi-
tions any," Mr. Reed explained.

"But if you were leading him, it would be all right,
wouldn't it?" she said. "Oh, please?"

Her father shrugged and looked at Mr. Reed. "I don't
suppose it would do any harm," Mr. Reed said.

Mr. Reed put his arm around her and swung her up
onto Little Red. The pony grunted and tossed his head
as she slid onto his back, and then stood still. Mr. Reed
took hold of the halter and Little Red moved quietly
along beside him. Without any saddle, Little Red's
back was slippery. He was not big and broad like the
work horses, and Nan had to dig her knees into his sides
to keep from slipping off. She wound the fingers of one
hand into his mane and then, with the other hand, waved
proudly to her mother on the porch. She began to like
the slippery feeling and the warmness of Little Red's
neck under her hand. She wished it was a long way to
the horse barn.

Just outside the barnyard gate, the overflow from the
watering trough made a muddy spot which stayed dark
brown and damp, even in dry weather. As they passed
the watering trough, Nan saw two pigeons waddling
through the mud to cool their feet. When the pigeons
saw Little Red, they flew up with a whir of wings, almost
in front of his nose. Little Red reared back in fright so

quickly that for a moment Mr. Reed lost his hold on the halter, and Nan found herself slipping down the pony's back. Then Little Red's front feet dropped to the ground, and before Nan had time to get settled again, Little Red kicked out with his hind feet, bucking fiercely up and down. With the first buck, Nan was thrown onto the pony's neck. She felt Mr. Reed grab her arm, but before he could get a good grip Little Red bucked again, and Nan went sprawling over the pony's head into the mud.

For a moment Nan lay perfectly still, with the breath knocked out of her. She couldn't breathe, and she couldn't scream. She could hear the pony and Mr. Reed moving above her, and she wanted to scramble out of the way, but she couldn't move. Then she rolled over and sat up. She brushed mud out of her eyes and was spitting mud out of her mouth when her father reached her. He set her on her feet and looked at her anxiously.

"You all right?" he asked.

She nodded, still spitting mud.

Then her father's anxious face cleared and he began to chuckle. "Well, you sure are a sight," he said, covering his mouth with his hand and trying not to laugh.

In an instant, all the hurt unhappy feelings in Nan turned to anger. She pounded her father's legs with her fists doubled up hard. "You don't have to laugh!" she

screamed. "I'll never ride that pony again. Never! Never! Never!" She stamped her foot and ran for the house, crying.

Her mother helped her out of her wet dirty clothes and into a bath full of warm water. She had just finished dressing, and was rinsing her mouth out with water for the third time, when she heard her father come into the kitchen.

"Where is she?" he asked.

"I told you that pony would hurt that child," Mrs. Coburn said.

"That didn't hurt her much. It just scared her in good shape."

"Just because she was lucky this time . . ." Mrs. Coburn said, ominously. "She said she'd never ride him again, and it will suit me if she never does."

"Well, she's going to ride him right now, as soon as she's cleaned up and dressed."

"Not tonight!" Mrs. Coburn exclaimed. "It's almost dark and she's still scared."

Mr. Coburn looked up and saw Nan standing in the kitchen doorway. "Well, you're looking better—cleaner, anyway."

"You didn't need to laugh," Nan said, but she wasn't angry now. She was just saying it for something to say.

"How about coming out for a ride on your pony now? Gramp is holding him, waiting for you."

Nan shook her head, tracing little designs on the wood floor with her toe.

"You don't want to be scared of a pony," her father said.

"I'm not scared any more. I just don't want to ride him. Ever." The frightened feeling inside Nan had changed; she could feel the difference. She wasn't hot-scared, angry-scared, running-away-scared, any more. She was cold scared now. She didn't want to think about Little Red. She wished he would go away and she would never have to ride a pony again.

"The longer it takes you to get back on, the harder it will be," Mr. Coburn said. "We should have put you right back on, as soon as you fell off, even if you were muddy and wet, before you had time to think about being scared. You get back on and ride, tonight, and in a week or two, you'll have forgotten you ever fell off."

For a moment Nan thought about Little Red, the warm feeling of him and the soft brown eyes when he wasn't scared and skittish. But then she remembered the way he had reared and bucked and the unsafe feeling she had had when she tried to hang on and knew she was going to fall.

Her father took her hand, "Come on," he said, "before it gets any darker."

Little Red was saddled and bridled. Her grandfather

was sitting on an upturned barrel, his cane hooked
through the pony's reins.

"Well, there's your pony," he said. "Now let's see you
get on and ride. Not every day a girl gets a new pony.
Better get in one ride before it gets dark."

He didn't even seem to know that she had fallen off,
Nan thought. Maybe he hadn't been watching; maybe
nobody had told him. Now he was looking at the pony,
as pleased as he had been at the Fair, waiting for her to
ride. With the saddle, it would be easier to stay on, she
thought. Maybe she *could* do it. But when she walked
over to Little Red, he switched his tail and stepped
sideways in a little dance, and Nan moved away again.

Her grandfather hooked his cane tighter in Little
Red's reins and pulled the pony up close to the barrel.

"Your Dad put a check rein on him—you don't need
it really, but it keeps him from bucking. It holds his
head up and if he can't get his head down, he can't
buck much. Did you ever notice that? Well, better be
getting on. Take him down to the barn and back a
couple of times and then we'll have to put him up."

Almost before she knew it, her father had lifted her
into the saddle. Nan grasped the reins with one hand
and the saddle horn with the other and worked her toes
into the stirrups.

"Both hands on the reins," her grandfather said.

Carefully she let go the saddle horn and took a good grip on the reins. Then she clucked to the pony and gently pressed her heels against his ribs and he moved off at a steady walk. On the first trip down to the barn and back, Nan sat very stiff and still, ready to grab for the saddle if the pony began to act up. As she turned for the second trip, her grandfather said, "Is that as fast as he can go?"

Nan was too busy to bother to answer. She could feel the pony surge forward as they started toward the barn. He knew there was hay in the barn and he was in a hurry to get back to it. She pulled in on the reins. He strained against them and trotted. She pulled harder and he settled back into a walk. Suddenly she realized that she had made him walk when he wanted to trot. She had decided what he should do and he had done it. Then she felt good again. She liked riding Little Red. He was her pony. When she turned around at the mud puddle and headed back toward her grandfather, she increased the pressure of her knees and clucked at Little Red, who obediently broke into a trot. She pulled up beside her grandfather and her father.

"He's okay now," she said.

4

A Loose Strap

Next morning at school Nan could hardly wait to tell everyone about Little Red. Miss Dunbar let her have first turn to talk at sharing time, and all the other children listened. Except Jean. Jean raised her hand for permission and then went out to the coat room to get a handkerchief, and she stayed all the time Nan was talking. At first Nan was too excited, talking and answering the other children's questions, to wonder why Jean wasn't there. But later, during arithmetic class, she thought about it and was sad that Jean had missed hearing about Little Red. Jean was her best friend—at least, sometimes Jean was her best friend. Other times Jean wouldn't play with her, or even talk to her, but just walked away whenever she came near, and then Nan felt sad and stuffy inside, as if she had eaten too much candy.

At recess Nan looked for Jean and tried to tell her about Little Red. Jean tossed the hair out of her eyes and wrinkled up her nose disgustedly. "It's only a pony," she said. "Who cares about ponies?" And then she went to play with the fourth grade girls.

Nan kicked up the dirt, wishing Jean would stay and hear about Little Red. It was no fun when the person to whom you most wanted to tell something wouldn't listen. For several minutes, Nan used the toe of her shoe to trace the outline of a pony in the dust. When she looked up again, she found that Rebecca Snow was standing near her, looking at her as if she wanted to say something. For a moment Nan had the feeling that she could tell Rebecca all about Little Red—how she and her grandfather had chosen him, and even how she had fallen in the mud when she first rode him. But before she could say anything, Rebecca blushed and then ducked her head and moved off. Then Nan was crosser with Rebecca than she had been with Jean. People shouldn't stand there and almost ask you to talk to them and then go away as soon as you looked at them.

For the next few days, after school, Nan rode Little Red up and down the lane from the barn to the pasture. At first she was very careful and sometimes she had to grab the saddle horn when Little Red started to trot. But each day she went farther up the lane and made Little Red go faster. And then one day, she knew she wasn't frightened at all any more. She leaned over Little Red's neck and spoke to him and gave him a little kick with her heels, and he was off, racing up the lane. The wind made tears in her eyes. Leaning low over his neck, she could feel the smooth powerful flow of the pony's muscles under her. It was like flying. When they got home, she gave Little Red an apple and stood for a long time, just leaning on him and thinking how wonderful he was.

That evening, Mrs. Coburn said, "Why haven't you asked Jean to come and see Little Red? All the rest of your friends have been here to see him."

Nan nibbled at the ends of her fingers and began to explain. "I tried to ask her. But she wouldn't listen. Whenever I talk about Little Red she just walks away."

"Maybe she's frightened," her mother said. "Growing up in the city, the way she did, she's not as used to animals as you are."

Nan nodded. Once Jean had run screaming into the house when she had seen a garden snake, and she didn't even like ladybugs. She said they made her feel squeamy. "But she won't even listen," Nan said. "She just walks away, and I don't think that's very nice. It isn't polite."

"Well, I don't think she means to be rude," Mrs. Coburn said. "She always has such nice manners."

Nan sighed. Jean was always especially polite to grownups. She talked in a soft voice and she seemed to know just what to say. She had special dresses with frills and smocking, which she always managed to keep clean, and all the mothers thought she was wonderful.

Nan had tried but she couldn't explain to her mother how sometimes it was exciting and fun to play with Jean—more fun than playing with anyone else—but other times she would cry or go home if you didn't play just what she wanted and let her be princess all day, while you did what she said. Mrs. Coburn always seemed to think Nan was the one at fault if Jean cried.

After school the next day, Nan waited for Jean in the hall. When she came out she was swinging her book bag and humming softly; she didn't say a word to Nan or even look at her. Nan followed her out and down the steps.

"Aren't you ever going to come and see my pony?" Nan called after her.

Jean turned around and smiled a secret sort of smile. "I might," she said softly.

"Well, when?" Nan asked.

"Oh, sometime," Jean said. "But ponies are so small."

"Little Red is a big pony."

"But not very big compared to a horse," Jean said. "I think horses are better for riding. My aunt has lots of horses, and I won a prize once with one of her horses, riding in a horse show."

"A prize!" Nan's eyes widened incredulously. "What sort of a prize?"

"A cup, silly, a gold cup, and its got my name cut right in the gold."

"I thought you were scared of animals," Nan said.

"Oh, pooh. My aunt's horses are specially trained, English style. They neck rein. If you want to ride them, you have to really know how to ride. Then it's easy. I guess your pony doesn't neck rein, does she?"

"It's a he—Little Red is a he," Nan said, and already Little Red seemed to be losing some of the magic importance he had for her.

"Well, I guess he doesn't neck rein."

"No—oo," Nan admitted, reluctantly.

"Well, if you want to walk home with me, I'll show you the cup I won," Jean said.

When they reached Jean's house, she stopped on the porch and put her finger to her lips. "My mother doesn't like me to brag about it, so be quiet now and don't tell anyone I showed you." They tiptoed into the living room, and Jean pushed a chair over to the bookcase and carefully took down a small shining gold cup. She held it out in her hand for Nan to see.

"You mustn't handle it," Jean said. "You might drop it."

Nan looked up and read the words engraved on the cup. "Norma Jean Ross," it said. "First Prize, Intermediate Class, Allington Horse Show."

"That's my real name—but everyone has always called me Jean."

She put the cup carefully in place and got down.

"That's wonderful," Nan said, trying not to feel jealous, but inside she knew that her pony world had lost a little of its specialness.

Jean smiled happily and took Nan's hand. "Come on, now. Let's play. I'll play anything you want—you choose." Jean was in a good mood now and it was one of the times when she made Nan feel that she was the best playmate in the world. All that afternoon they played happily. Jean agreed to play hopscotch, which she usually didn't like, and said, "Good for you," without getting angry when Nan won. Then they played cowboys and Indians with the Connor boys across the way, and Jean never once said she was tired or teased Nan to go inside and play dress-up. When it was suppertime, Jean walked part way home with Nan and they held each other's hands and sang, "Do not step on a crack, or you'll break your mother's back," skipping along the squares of the sidewalk.

"I like Jean," Nan said at the supper table.

"I'm glad," her mother said. "I like to have you play with her. She's such a nice girl."

Then Nan almost told about Jean's prize cup, but she remembered in time that Jean had asked her not to tell anyone.

For the next week, Jean and Nan played together nearly every day at Jean's house. One day Jean took

Nan up to her room and showed her two new dresses and a winter coat with fur on the collar. "My father bought them for me," she said, as she rubbed the blue velvet jumper against her cheek. "I like this one best. My mother told my father he was too extravagant. But I think it's nice to have a father that is too extravagant, don't you?"

Nan nodded, but she wished that Jean would stop thinking about dresses and come with her to see Little Red, even if he wasn't a horse and didn't neck rein. But Jean didn't want to.

Then one day Bob Connor was playing with the girls and he asked Nan to let him ride on her pony. At first Jean didn't want to go, but Nan said, "I went and looked at your dresses." And she was pleased when Jean said, "Oh, all right. I suppose we might as well go."

When they reached the farm, Bob went in with Nan to watch her brush Little Red. He brought the saddle and helped cinch the girth. Then Nan showed him how she could make Little Red open his mouth to take in the bit, when she put her thumb in, right at the back of his lip, where he had no teeth.

Bob led Little Red outside.

"Are you going to ride first?" he asked Nan.

Little Red was frisky. He hadn't had much exercise, standing in the barn all the days that Nan had been playing with Jean. Nan got on and before she was hardly settled in the saddle, Little Red whirled and started off down the lane at a gallop. Nan leaned over his neck and worked on the reins until he slowed to a trot. Next he shied sideways at a pile of rustling leaves, and for a moment Nan felt as scared as she had the first time she rode him. She gripped him tighter with her knees and spoke softly to him until he stopped dancing skittishly and began to trot again. Then she rode him four or five times up and down the lane, and when he was going easily, she took him back to where the other children were waiting under the lilac tree.

"You want a turn now?" she asked Bob. "He's quieting down all right."

"Sure. Sure I do," Bob said, grinning with excitement.

Nan watched the easy way Bob swung onto the pony and how he held the pony to a trot as he started down the lane. Her father had told her she must be careful when other children rode Little Red, but she thought Bob could ride as well as she could. He must have done a lot of riding, she thought.

Bob rode twice more up and down the lane, and while she was watching him, Nan saw Rebecca Snow walking slowly along at the end of the lane. Before she had quite gone out of sight, she stopped and leaned against the fence. She had her back turned to the children, but Nan thought she was looking at them out of the corner of her eye. Nan was curious about Rebecca. Usually

Rebecca hurried away from school as soon as the final bell rang. She lived a long way out in the country, Nan knew, and she always seemed to be in a hurry. But today she was late going home. Nan noticed, now, that she had a brown paper bag in one hand. Probably she had stopped at the store, Nan thought. It suddenly occurred to Nan that Rebecca might like to have a ride on Little Red. I'll ask her, Nan thought, but before she did anything about it, Bob interrupted her. He slid off the pony and stood with his arm over Little Red's neck.

"He's all right," he said, admiringly.

"You can ride again, if you want," Nan said. "He needs some more exercise."

"It's Jean's turn now," Bob said.

"But he's so little," Jean argued. "I'm used to riding a horse."

"He's big enough," Bob told her. "He'll carry you, all right."

"Well, suppose I don't feel like riding," Jean teased.

"Be a sport," Bob urged. "Come on."

Bob grabbed her by the arms and tried to drag her to the pony. Jean dug in her heels and giggled and then went limp.

"Aw, come on," Bob said.

For a moment Jean sat still on the grass; then suddenly she scrambled up, smiling. "All right," she said.

Little Red kept on contentedly grubbing in the grass while Jean got on. She pulled gently on the reins, and when the pony failed to respond, she dropped the reins back over the saddle. "Poor thing, he doesn't want to go," she said. "I'll get off and let him rest." She shifted her weight in the saddle, starting to get off.

"That's okay—I'll get him started," Bob said. He made a loud clucking noise and reached out to pull up on the reins.

Little Red snapped his head up and moved sideways away from Bob's hand.

"Look out," Nan shouted, but she was too late. Jean grabbed for the saddle horn, but with her weight all on one side, the saddle began to slip. The saddle girth loosened and as Nan watched, the saddle turned all the way under the pony's belly. Jean's shoulders were almost touching the ground but her foot, still caught in the stirrup, held her prisoner. If Little Red panicked and ran now, she would be hurt. Nan wanted to rush to Little Red, to get hold of the bridle. But she knew he was frightened already. She could see the muscles in his neck twitch. One sudden move and he would run, she knew. She motioned Bob back and then took a small step forward. Jean began to scream and the pony moved restlessly.

"Be quiet, Jean," Nan said in a low intense voice.

Miraculously this time Jean, who never heard what other children said, seemed to hear Nan and stopped in the middle of the scream. Nan took another step forward and another. Slowly she extended her hand, palm upward, as though she was bringing him sugar. "Okay, boy," she whispered. And then she had one hand on Little Red's nose and the other on the bridle. She heaved a long sigh as Bob got Jean's foot out of the stirrup and dragged her away from the pony. All at once Nan felt weak and trembly. "It was my fault," Nan said, almost to herself. "I should have thought to tighten the saddle girth again."

For a moment, Jean lay on the grass, her face white and scared.

"Are you hurt?" Bob asked. "Are you all right?"

Jean stared straight ahead and instead of answering, she began to scream. She turned over on her stomach and screamed louder and louder. Nan looked for a place to hitch the pony, but before she found one, Rebecca was standing beside her. "I'll hold him," she said quietly, and took the reins. Nan nodded and ran to Jean.

"Jean!" she shouted. "Are you hurt?" Still screaming, Jean turned over and pounded Nan with her fists. Then she grabbed Nan's arm and bit hard into the flesh.

"You did it," she screamed. "You wanted me to fall off. You made the saddle slip."

Nan got up, holding her arm with the other hand. There were two rows of tooth marks, red and puffy already, and they hurt. Jean had started to scream again, and now Mrs. Coburn was coming down the path from the house and Bob was rushing back from the barn, carrying a pail of water. Bob reached them just ahead of Mrs. Coburn and before anyone could stop him, he dumped the pail of water over Jean's head.

"What's the matter? What in the world is going on?" Mrs. Coburn asked.

When the water hit her, Jean stopped in the middle of a scream. She still made whimpering noises under her breath and her eyes were dark and frightened, but she had stopped screaming.

Bob set down the pail and he looked white and scared too. For a moment none of them said anything, and then they were all talking at once, telling Mrs. Coburn what had happened, how the saddle had slipped, and how Nan had managed to get hold of the pony, how Jean had bitten Nan when Nan was only trying to help, how Bob had heard someone say that when people were hys— hys—well whatever it was, screaming and behaving that way, the best thing was to throw water on them.

"Anyway, it worked," he said, shaking his head apologetically. "But it sure made an awful splash."

Mrs. Coburn had Jean in her arms now, and over Jean's shoulder, she shook her head sadly at them.

"Poor girl," she said to Jean. "I'll get you into some dry clothes and then take you home."

In the excitement Nan had forgotten Little Red. Now she turned and found him standing quietly beside Rebecca, who had her hand on his nose and was talking to him. When Nan went over to them, Rebecca quickly handed over the reins. "Thanks," Nan said. "Thanks for holding him, and getting him quieted down too."

Rebecca ducked her head. "It's okay," she said. "And it wasn't your fault—what happened." Then she turned and hurried off down the road. When she was out of sight, Nan remembered that she had been going to ask her if she'd like a ride on Little Red.

At supper Nan waited for someone else to bring up the incident of the afternoon. At last when supper was finished, her father pushed back his chair and looked at her. "Did you have a bit of trouble today?" he asked.

Nan nodded, miserably.

"You must always be sure to look at the saddle and see that it's cinched tight, especially when any other children are riding. And you ought to be particularly careful with someone like Jean, who has never ridden before."

"But she has ridden," Nan assured him. "She's ridden a lot on her aunt's horses. She even won a prize once in a horse show."

"Huh," said her father, shaking his head, "I guess if she told you that, she must have been fibbing."

"No, it wasn't a fib; it was true. I saw the cup—gold— and it had her name on it."

"Oh, Nan, did she tell you that was her cup?" her mother asked. "Mrs. Ross showed me that cup once. It's a cup Jean's aunt won, years ago, even before Jean was born. It's her Aunt Norma's cup, not hers at all."

Her mother thought for a minute. "Nan," she said, "if she told you all that, then you weren't so much at fault as I thought. You didn't know she was frightened. And if she hadn't been frightened and trying to get off, the saddle probably wouldn't have slipped. Poor Jean. And poor Nan. It was a fright for you too."

Nan nodded and she felt almost like crying. She went over and sat down on her mother's knee. Poor Jean, she thought, she doesn't really have any riding prize, and I really *do* have Little Red. She felt sorry for Jean. She couldn't make Jean get on and ride again, the way her father had made her, so that she wouldn't be scared any more. Not unless Jean wanted to, and Nan didn't think she would. But she knew one thing she could do.

"I won't ever tell anyone at school about Jean making up the story about a riding prize," Nan said.

Her mother smiled and gave her a big hug.

5

The Nuisance

For some time after Jean's fall, she and Nan did not play together very much. Nan spent most of her time after school riding Little Red. Sometimes Bob came home with her and they took turns with the pony. But more often Nan rode alone. Sometimes she rode high up into the pasture woods, following cow paths that were filled with dry leaves that made a whishing sound when Little Red walked through them.

Then late in November, it began to snow. At first there was only a little snow in a thin layer on the ground, with brown stalks of weeds and hummocks of grass showing through it. It looked the way Nan's cake had looked once when she made a white icing that was too thin. There was so little snow that Little Red could trot along on it with no trouble. But even in her mittens, Nan's hands got cold holding the reins.

Then one morning Nan woke up and the whole world outside her window was white. The tree branches were white, the ground was white, and the air was filled with the lacy pattern of falling snowflakes. The hummocks of grass were mounded over now, and the tops of the fence posts were capped with snow. Even the barking of the dog and her father's voice in the farmyard seemed muffled, and when those noises stopped everything was quiet, as if the world had gone far away and left her on a silent island of snow.

When it was time to get ready for school, Mrs. Coburn brought out Nan's woolen snow suit, with leggings and a jacket. The jacket was dark blue, with a band of red on the collar and pockets, and she had a red and white knitted ski cap and red boots. It took a long time to get into so many clothes, but they were warm and cosy, and on the way to school Nan liked to pretend that she was an arctic explorer, on an expedition to the North Pole.

Just as she was leaving for school, she thought of something. "Dad, will I be able to ride Little Red in all this snow?" she asked.

"He'll be all right in the snow, Nan," Mr. Coburn said. "But you'll have to keep him off the road when it's icy."

"You drive the big horses on the road with the sleigh," Nan pointed out.

"Sure, but their feet are shod, and Little Red's aren't. And even the big horses have to have special shoeing for the ice. The blacksmith puts four sharp metal spikes—corks, he calls them—into each shoe. Sort of like the kind mountain climbers use. Without them, Little Red might fall and break a leg on the ice."

That afternoon, Nan got her sled down from the attic, but before she went up to the hill, she stopped at the barn to see Little Red. During the fall, his coat had grown thick, to keep him warm in the cold weather, and even when Nan brushed and curried him, he still looked patchy, like someone who has just gotten out of bed, with his hair sticking out in all directions. Nan patted him and gave him a piece of her apple. When she turned away, Little Red nickered and pushed restlessly against the door of his stall. He was used to going with her and didn't like being left.

"No, boy," Nan said. The road was already getting icy from the car tires and sleigh runners. It was just what made good sliding, but it wasn't good for Little Red.

Once or twice Nan took Little Red out into the field in the weeks that followed, and tried riding him there, but it wasn't much fun. There were deep drifts in the fields which frightened Little Red. When he felt himself settling down into the snow, he jumped and kicked to free himself. Nan made a path with a shovel and rode Little Red back and forth on it, but after a few days, there was a thaw and then another freeze and after that the path was as icy as the road. Finally Nan gave up trying to ride Little Red. She went to see him almost every day and took him apples, but it wasn't the same as riding him. Sometimes she was so busy, sliding and skiing, that she only saw Little Red at feeding time.

One morning Mr. Coburn came in from the barn, looking cross.

"That durned pony," he said, "doesn't get enough exercise. And he eats almost as much as a horse."

"What did he do now?" Mrs. Coburn asked.

"Do?" Mr. Coburn shouted. "He stuck his nose right through a pane of glass. That's what he did. I was leading him out to the watering trough and he just stopped and poked his nose right through the window. And then he grinned at me!"

Nan laughed. "He couldn't really grin at you."

Mr. Coburn almost smiled back at her, and when he spoke he didn't sound quite so cross. "Well, it looked like a grin to me," he said.

"What did you do?" Nan asked.

"Huh! I put a bran sack in the window to keep out the wind. But I'll tell you what I'll do if he does that many more times. I'll sell that pony. He's more bother than a dozen horses."

"But he never did anything bad before," Nan said.

"I'll tell you what he did," Mr. Coburn said. "Last week he got out of his stall somehow and spilled a bag of grain. Ate what he wanted and then dragged the bag around, spilling it all over the place. And you were too busy sliding and skiing, even to take him out to water. That's the trouble. He's got so much energy stored up, he just thinks up some kind of devilment to use it up. Just like a child."

Nan sighed. "I'll take him out in the yard more," she promised. "That will give him some exercise."

One morning a few days later, Nan woke very early while it was still dark outside. Mrs. Coburn was standing by the bed, gently shaking her and calling her name.

"Nan, are you awake?"

"Ummm," Nan said sleepily.

"Nan, your grandfather's sick," her mother said. "The doctor has just been here, and he thinks it's pneumonia. And your father has a bad cold too. I want you to get dressed and help with the chores. Your father will do the milking. But you can help by watering the horses."

As soon as she stuck her feet out of bed, the chill air of the room woke her up. And once she was awake another chill struck through her too. She remembered once before her grandfather had been sick with pneumonia. She remembered her parents' worried faces and the queer silence in the house which made the familiar rooms seem strange, as though she was living in someone else's house by mistake. Now while she got dressed, she thought about her grandfather, and she was afraid.

There was only one thing she could do. She would hurry up and help her father so that he would not get pneumonia too. She left her flannel pajamas on and put a heavy sweater on under her snow suit. Even so, when she stepped out into the dark yard, she felt the cold stab through her clothes. Fifteen below zero, the thermometer outside the kitchen window said. She was glad to get into the horse barn and lean against Little Red's warm furry side. She slipped the rope through his halter and led him out of the barn. At the watering shed she held the end of the rope and waited for Little Red to drink. He put his head down to the trough and blew and snorted, but he didn't drink. Nan leaned over the trough and in the dim light she could just see the blue silvery ice that covered it over. Quickly she took Little Red back to the horse barn and hitched him to the ring just inside the door.

Then she ran to the house. She knew what to do; she had seen her father do it many times. First she took an old black kettle and put paper and chips and kindling in the bottom and ran back to the watering trough with it. She set it under the water pipe and lit the kindling with a match she brought from the house. She ran back to the wood shed for some bigger sticks and when the fire was burning well, she added the wood. Then she went back to the shed for the hatchet and began to chop at the ice in the trough. When she had chopped several inches of ice, the hatchet broke through and sent drops of icy water into her face. After that every stroke of the hatchet covered her with an icy spray, but she had to keep on chopping until she had made a hole big enough for the horses to drink.

By the time the hole seemed big enough, Nan could see the lemon yellow squares of light from the cowbarn, where her father was starting to milk the cows. Now the whole world seemed to be turning blue; the snow was a purply-blue and the sky was a deep navy blue, not the light blue of daytime. In a few minutes now, the sun's first rays would reach the top of the hill beyond the house, and Nan knew which trees the sun would touch first. Over the house she could see the smoke rising from the kitchen chimney, rising straight up in the still cold air.

"Well, how is my helper getting along?" Her father's voice surprised her.

"Okay—I guess," she said, looking doubtfully at the hole she had made.

"Here, let me give you a hand." With three or four strokes of the hatchet, Mr. Coburn made the hole twice as big as it had been. Then he set two pieces of wood under the kettle so that the fire came close up under the pipe.

"It will start running before too long now. Just this little part freezes, here where it's exposed to the air. Now, do you think you can water the horses?" he asked.

She nodded and he picked up the milk pails and went on toward the house. Nan listened to the squeak and crunch of the snow under his feet, and then she thought about winter sounds—the creaking of frozen branches, and the tinkle of icy twigs hitting against each other in the wind. While she was thinking, Nan heard another tinkling sound, closer at hand. It must be ice shattering from the larger branches of the elms, she thought. Then suddenly she realized that it was not ice at all. It was glass. She turned and ran toward the horse barn. Little Red was no longer hitched near the door. He was standing in front of the window, and he *was* grinning; his lips were turned back from his teeth and his eyes positively twinkled. Under his feet there were shattered pieces of glass and the bottom two rows of the window frame were empty—he had knocked out eight panes of glass.

"Oh, Little Red! How could you do such a thing!" Nan cried.

Quickly Nan led Little Red and the horses out for their water. Then she found old grain sacks and stuffed them into the window as well as she could and followed her father into the house.

"Guess what?" Nan said, while she was pulling off her boots.

"The water started running?" Mr. Coburn said, grinning.

"No. That is, I don't know. I didn't look."

"Well, what then? Whatever it is, you don't look very happy about it."

Nan swallowed. "It's terrible," she said. "Little Red got loose while I was chopping the ice and broke two rows of glass out of the window."

"Eight panes of glass!" Mr. Coburn said, and the smile was gone from his face now.

Nan nodded; she felt she might cry if she tried to say anything more.

Her father looked grim. "I won't have that pony around the place if he keeps making such a nuisance of himself!"

Nan sniffed back the tears. "Pr-pretty soon it will be spring and I—I can ride him again. Then he won't break any more windows."

"Then I suppose he'll get loose and run around out in the fields and trample down all the grass before I can get it mowed."

Nan put her head down and began to cry.

Mr. Coburn coughed. "Well, I'll have to go and get some glass and fix it, that's all."

"I pp-put some s-sacks in," Nan sobbed.

"Sacks won't keep the cold out much in weather like this." Mr. Coburn jammed his feet into his boots and stalked out.

Even though it was Saturday, Nan stayed away from the barn all day. She didn't want to see the shiny new panes of glass. She didn't want to think what would happen if Little Red got loose again and poked his nose through *them*. She wished she could go and talk to her grandfather, but her mother said he was too sick to talk. When Nan stood outside his door, she could hear his voice, so thick and unsteady that it didn't sound like his ordinary voice at all. And again the cold chill of fear gripped her. Her grandfather had always been there. He was a part of her life. He teased her, sometimes, but he seemed to know how she felt about things, too, and lots of times he helped her out when things went wrong. If anything happened to him—

The whole world seemed unhappy and nothing was right today. Instead of working around the barn, her father was sitting in a rocker with his feet up on the front of the kitchen stove. He was reading a book, right in the middle of the day, and his voice sounded almost as bad as her grandfather's. Late in the afternoon, the doctor came to see her grandfather again. He was in the room for a long time, and Nan wondered whether he was doing something that would make her grandfather better. Her father kept his eyes on his book, and for a long time Nan sat in a corner near the stove and wished he would talk to her about her grandfather or say something to show he wasn't cross any more.

At last he looked at her out of the corner of his eye.

"Something bothering you, Old Top?" he asked.

Nan didn't trust her voice. She nodded.

"Something about that window maybe?"

Nan nodded again.

"You don't want to take it too much to heart. Maybe I was too cross this morning. Anyway it's all fixed now, and nothing to worry about."

"I was thinking—what if he did it again!" Nan said.

"Oh, that! I've fixed it this time so that Little Red won't ever do that again. You go and take a look."

In a minute Nan had slipped on her jacket and boots and was on her way out of the house. She wondered what her father had done. Maybe he'd put a sort of muzzle on Little Red, like the ones you put on dogs. Or a poke, a big wooden poke that cows wear around their necks so that they can't push through between the wires and get out of the pasture. She didn't see how that would keep Little Red from poking his nose through windows, though, and she did hope Little Red didn't have a poke. It would be so heavy and make him feel dreadful, she knew.

She went through the shed and directly into the horse barn, and when she reached Little Red's stall, she looked him over and he didn't have a poke or a muzzle or anything else different that she could see. She patted him and rubbed her face against his neck.

"You must never, never put your nose through windows again," she said severely.

He whinnied softly, and she thought he gave his head the slightest up and down nod, as though he understood.

Next Nan went over to look at the new window and then she discovered what her father had done. Across the lower part of the window he had nailed wooden bars, so close together that not even a pony could get his nose through.

"Oh, thank you," Nan said under her breath and then dashed back to the house. She burst into the kitchen and hugged her father. He put down the book he was reading and grinned at her.

"I think we've got that nuisance stopped this time, don't you?" he asked. She nodded.

Then Mr. Coburn said, "The doctor says your grandfather is a lot better. It's not pneumonia after all—nothing worse than a bad cold. You can go and see him now if you want to." Then he added, "Tell him about Little Red and the window. That will cheer him up."

6

Tit for Tat

After Mr. Coburn put the wooden bars on the windows, Little Red didn't have a chance to make a nuisance of himself any more, but Nan knew that he was tired of standing in the barn. She was glad when spring came and the snow melted, so that she could take him out again.

At first Little Red was frisky and hard to handle. He jumped sideways and danced up and down when he saw a piece of paper blowing along the side of the road. And one day, he ran away with Nan. He ran all the way from the schoolyard, with his legs stretched out, ta-da-da, ta-da-da, through the village and home to the barn. Nan had pulled on the reins at first, but then she had to hold on to the saddle with both hands to keep from falling off. When Little Red stopped in front of the barnyard gate, he threw his head over the top of the gate and no matter how hard she pulled on the reins, or kicked him in the sides with her heels, he wouldn't move.

For a moment Nan was scared and shaky. Then she began to feel angry. She pulled hard on one rein until Little Red's head came around. He turned a complete circle and put his head back over the fence. Nan was starting to pull his head around again, when she heard her grandfather's voice close by.

"Well, he gave you a run for your money, didn't he?" her grandfather asked.

Nan nodded. "First he ran away, and now he won't go at all," she said.

"Here's something that might help—something I thought you might be needing." Her grandfather held out a braided leather quirt. At one end there was a loop to go over her wrist, and at the other end there were three narrow strips of leather about six inches long. He showed Nan how to hold the quirt when she wasn't using it, and then he showed her how she could snap the three leather thongs. They made a sharp cracking sound and when Little Red heard it, he lifted his head, his ears pricked up and his nostrils widened.

"See, that makes him look lively," her grandfather chuckled.

"Won't he run away?" Nan asked doubtfully.

"Not if you keep the bit tight in his mouth, the way it ought to be." He leaned over and tightened a strap on the bridle. "He got the bit between his teeth before, and that was why you couldn't stop him. But tightening up that strap should take care of that."

"Now, you carry this," her grandfather continued, "and if he doesn't go, you snap it in the air, or give him a touch of it under the belly. It won't take much, and pretty soon he'll know who is the boss. A horse has to know who is boss. He's either going to do what he wants to do, or he's going to do what you want to do. Today he's been doing what *he* wants. Now you make him do what *you* want."

Right then, Nan wasn't very sure what she did want. She wished she could just put Little Red in the barn and not ride any more, at least not for a while, but her grandfather was standing back, waiting to see her put Little Red through his paces. She flicked the quirt against Little Red's flank, and he lifted his leg and swished his tail.

"Harder than that," her grandfather said.

With one hand Nan pulled back hard on the reins, and with the other she flicked Little Red again harder. To her surprise, Little Red swung away from the gate and began to walk down the yard. She flicked him again, still holding the reins tight. He jumped and bucked, uneasily, and then settled into a slow, even trot. She took him out to the corner of the road and back, and when he tried to go up to the gate, she flicked him again and turned him around neatly in front of her grandfather.

"It works!" she said.

"Of course it works," he said.

"But doesn't it hurt him?" she asked.

"Not if you use it right. Oh, it stings him a little. That's what makes him pay attention. But after you've used it a few times, if you just carry it, and maybe snap it in the air, you won't even have to touch him with it. He'll remember."

For the rest of the afternoon, Little Red went where she wanted him to, and after she had put him in his stall, Nan stood in the yard and snapped her quirt in the air. She liked the smooth brown handle and the smell of leather, like new shoes. Once she had seen a trained pony doing tricks on the vaudeville stage at the fair. A lady in jodhpurs had been with him, and when she snapped her whip once, he rolled over and when she snapped it again, he rolled back and stood up and bowed his head three times. Nan wondered if she could train Little Red to do tricks.

Just then Mr. Coburn came through the yard, carrying the milk pails to the barn. "What have you got there?" he asked.

"A quirt," she said. "Gramp gave it to me. To make Little Red go."

Mr. Coburn set down the milk pails and took the quirt in his hands. He turned it over thoughtfully, felt the braided leather and snapped it several times.

"Yes," he said, "that's a nice little whip. It helps, sometimes, to have a whip, as long as you know how to use it."

"Oh, I know how," she said. "Gramp showed me, and I made Little Red do just what I wanted him to, all the rest of the afternoon."

Her father looked at her for a minute as if he were going to say something, but he only handed the quirt back to her and, whistling, took up the milk pails and went on toward the barn.

After that, Nan carried the quirt with her most of the time whether she was riding Little Red or not. She found she could flick flies off the porch rail with it and cut leaves off the lower branches of trees. She didn't often have to use it on Little Red, but now and then, when he put his head down to eat grass, she touched him with it lightly, and he shivered and pulled up his head and went on.

One Saturday morning after breakfast, Mr. Coburn stopped Nan as she was going out into the yard. "I've got a job I want you to do for me today," he said.

"Oh, golly," Nan moaned, "do I have to do it today?" Sometimes Nan liked to do errands for her father, but today she had been planning to play with Jean.

"It won't take more than an hour or two," her father said. "I've got all I can do today with the last of the corn to plant. And somebody's got to go up and find out whether the pasture spring needs cleaning out. Your mother thinks the water tastes funny, and if anything's fallen into the spring, we can shift over and use the water from the spring in the north meadow until I get time to clean the other spring out."

"But what could fall in the spring?" Nan asked. "There's a cover on it."

Her father looked at her and smiled. "Well, quite a few years ago, a woodchuck wiggled in under the cover. Once he got in, he couldn't get out, and finally he fell in the water and drowned."

Nan wrinkled up her nose in disgust. "Ooo," she said. "I don't think I'll drink any more water."

"That was a long time ago," Mr. Coburn said. "And I don't think you'll find anything in it this time. The new cover has a pretty tight fit. But it doesn't do any harm to check now and then."

"I still wish I didn't have to go," Nan muttered, but Mr. Coburn was hurrying off toward the barn and didn't hear her.

She was cross when she went out to saddle Little Red, and as though he knew it, he swelled up as fat as he could so that she had trouble getting the saddle girth tight.

"Naughty old thing!" she said. She pressed her knee against his side and pulled on the cinch strap as hard as she could, until finally it seemed tight enough. Then she led Little Red out into the yard, got on him and set out for the pasture. They climbed the first hill to the pasture gate. When Nan got off to let down the bars, the saddle slipped the way it had with Jean. Nan sat down very hard on the ground and although it didn't hurt her much, it made her crosser than she already was. She pulled the saddle girth tight and then led Little Red through the gate with a hard tug on the reins.

Just inside the gate, along the fence line, there was a large willow tree. The sun was getting hot and Nan was glad to stop in its shade. It was her grandfather's special tree. When he was a young man, he had put in some fence posts made of fresh willow, and one post had taken root and grown into this tree. The wires of the fence went right through the bark of the tree and came out on the other side. Every time Nan went that way, she stopped and looked at that tree and wondered if it could really have started from a fence post.

Soon Nan was ready to go on and they left the shade and followed a cow path which led them through bushes and along the side of a hill in a gradual climb. Most of the bushes they passed were barberry bushes, and Little Red pushed close to them, using them, as the cows did, to scratch himself and to scare off flies. Sometimes when they came too close, Nan curled her leg up over the saddle horn, but sometimes she forgot and then the thorns scratched her legs as she rode past. When they came to a particularly large thorny bush, Nan tried to pull Little Red to the other side of the path. Little Red took a few sideways steps and then lunged across the path toward the bush. Nan was thrown off balance and didn't have time to move her leg or lean away from the bush. Little Red pushed through the barberries and when they were past the bush, Nan discovered that she had deep scratches on her arms and legs. The scratches smarted and stung and they made her cross. She wished she didn't have to go all the way up to the spring.

They crossed the brook and began to climb up the last steep hill. At last they were at the top, and Little Red stopped. Nan got off and went over to the spring. She found a hinged cover and looked in. Below her, she could see the dark distant reflection of the walls of the spring in the water. When her eyes became accustomed to the darkness, she could see the stones shimmering far below the surface of the water. There was nothing in the spring that shouldn't be there, no twigs or leaves and certainly no dead animals. The water looked so cool and clear that she wished she could get a drink.

All that way for nothing, Nan thought. She was cross and hot, and it seemed to her that nothing had gone right all day. She got back on the pony and wished that he would hurry, but he picked his way slowly down the steep path, sliding occasionally on a loose rock and sending stones rattling down ahead of them.

At the brook at the bottom of the hill, Nan slipped off and found a clear pool of water where she could lie flat on her stomach on the grass and get a drink. The pony drank from another pool farther downstream. When she had finished, Nan pulled at Little Red's bridle. Her father had told her not to let a horse drink too much when he was hot. She pulled and pulled, but he paid no attention to her tugs; he just kept on drinking. She could see the muscles in his throat working under the smooth red-brown hair on his neck. She pulled at the reins harder, and then suddenly she felt very angry. He was drinking so much that he would be sick, and he wouldn't even stop when she tried to pull him away.

In her anger, almost without stopping to think, Nan took the quirt which she always carried dangling from her wrist and gave Little Red a hard cut across the flank with it. In an instant, his head came up, and before Nan knew what was happening, he whirled and kicked her. The kick hit her leg above the knee and she fell down. For a moment she lay still in the grass. She was no longer angry, and she wasn't exactly frightened either, but she was very much surprised. Slowly she sat up. Little Red was eating grass a little way down the hill, and he lifted

his head and gave a soft nicker and then went on eating. I suppose he's saying he's sorry, Nan thought. She felt her leg. It hurt but it seemed to work properly. She rolled up her pants and found a red hoof-shaped mark on her leg. Carefully, she stood up and when she found she could walk, she worked her way closer to Little Red. She wasn't sure now what he would do; perhaps he wouldn't let himself be caught.

"Here, boy," she said, softly.

Little Red lifted his head and looked at her. He switched his tail and then put his head down and began to eat again. She moved closer, wondering whether he would whirl and try to kick her again, or possibly just run away. She took another step forward and he lifted his head again. When he put his head down, she took another step, and this time he paid no attention. She moved slowly closer until she was able to reach out and get hold of his bridle. She put her arm over his neck and whispered, "I'm sorry I hit you." Then she got on and rode home.

After she had put Little Red in his stall, Nan went out and sat on the front step. It was made of one large piece of granite, and it was always cool, even on the hottest days. It was shaded by the larch tree and the house, and it always seemed to Nan that it kept the feel of snow; it was her favorite place to sit when it was hot. Everyone used the kitchen door or the side door; no one ever went in the front way, and with the house in back of her, and the larch tree overhead, and wild roses and ferns on either side of the doorstep, it was like a cool green cave of her very own.

But today even her cave didn't seem like a happy place. Nan was worrying. She was ashamed to tell the family about getting kicked. And she didn't know which part she was ashamed of most. She was ashamed that she had whipped Little Red when she was angry. But she was also ashamed that she hadn't held onto the bridle, so that he couldn't kick her.

At the lunch table, she waited for her father to ask her about the water in the spring. He seemed to have forgotten that he had asked her to go up there; he was busy talking about the hay in the lower field. At last he turned to her and said, "Well, did you get up to see about the spring?"

"It's all right," Nan said stiffly. "There's nothing in it."

"I didn't think there would be," he said. He turned to Mrs. Coburn. "You must have been tasting things that weren't there," he teased.

"It certainly did taste funny," she said.

"All in your imagination," Mr. Coburn said, but he touched her on the shoulder and smiled. Then he turned to Nan again. "It's a good thing to be sure about the spring," he said, "and I just about got the corn planting finished up while you were gone. So you really helped. And it wasn't such a bad trip, was it, after all?"

"It was a whole lot worse!" Nan said crossly. "It was hot and I got scratched on a barberry bush and Little Red kicked me."

"Can't you keep out of barberry bushes?" her father began in a teasing voice. Then he stopped. "Did you say Little Red kicked you? Where? Where did he kick you? And how did he happen to kick you?"

Nan rolled up her pants again and showed them the red welt on her leg. Then the whole story came tumbling out, and she was glad to get it told and over with. When she had finished, nobody said anything for a moment. Finally her father shook his head and said, "I thought you were handling that whip mighty free and easy."

"A whip is like any other dangerous tool," her grandfather said. "If you use it right, it's a good thing; but if you're careless, it can cause trouble." Then her grandfather smiled. "That's a hard way of learning how to use a whip," he said. "But I guess you have learned, all right."

Nan nodded. Beneath her rolled-up pants leg, she could see that the hoof mark on her leg was beginning to turn a purplish blue, but she didn't care. Now that every-body knew about it, she wasn't ashamed of it any more. It was just a hurt, like any other hurt, and in a few days it would go away.

7

A New Friend

By the time the black and blue mark from Little Red's kick had completely disappeared from Nan's leg, school was over and summer had come.

On the first day of vacation, Nan felt the wonderful freedom of a whole summer stretching out before her. She didn't have to get up and get dressed and rush off to school. She could take her time about things. She could watch her father sharpening scythes on the grindstone. She liked the steady burring sound, and sometimes her father sent her to fill the can that sent a trickle of water over the turning stone to keep it from getting too hot. Or she could go and see the sprigs of new lettuce coming up in a row in the garden, and pick a few radishes to see whether the biggest tops had the fattest radishes on them.

But this first morning Nan thought she would take Little Red and go for a long ride.

She packed sandwiches in a paper bag, and then she saddled Little Red and rode down to Connor's to see if Bob could go with her. Bob had a pony of his own now, an Indian pony, bigger than Little Red, that had come all the way from New Mexico, Bob said. And Bob had promised to go riding with her, as soon as school was out. But when she reached the Connor's, she found Bob and his mother just getting into the car. Bob couldn't go riding today, his mother said, because he had to go to the dentist's to get his teeth cleaned.

"I'd a lot rather go with you," Bob said, and made a grimace behind his mother's back as he got into the car.

Nan watched them drive off toward the city, and then she decided that she would go somewhere that she had never been before. She rode through town and out on the dirt road toward Brookford. When it seemed to her that she had ridden for a long time, she began to get hungry, and even though she could tell by the sun that it wasn't noon time yet, she looked for a grassy spot beside the road where Little Red could graze and then sat down on the bank and ate her sandwiches.

After she had eaten, Nan rode slowly on until she came to a fork in the road. One road led past the Hill Church, she knew. She had been that way many times in the car, when her family drove over the hill to visit friends in Brookford. For a moment, she couldn't remember where the other road led; she thought she had been down it once, a long time ago. Then suddenly she realized that this must be the road to Rebecca's house. The Snow's farm was at the end of the road. Nan hesitated. There was something strange and sad about Rebecca's family, Nan knew. She tried to remember what she had heard people say about them, but she couldn't. She only knew that she didn't want to go to the Snow's. She didn't know exactly why, but there was something frightening about them, and even Rebecca was so quiet that Nan never felt comfortable with her. But the road wound through some woods and the shade looked pleasant. Out in the sun, it was getting hot now. Nan decided she would ride just a little way into the woods and then turn back.

In the woods, the dark green shadows closed around her, and the speckled light of the sun, sifting through the tree tops, made a shifting pattern on the road. Ferns grew on the banks on either side, and there were red spots of wild columbine among the ferns. Nan gave Little Red his head, and they plodded on so slowly and peacefully that Nan almost went to sleep.

Then suddenly, she was aware of a splash of light. They were coming out of the woods into an open meadow, and before her, she saw a small weather-beaten farm house and beyond it sheds and a barn, all the gray-

brown color of weathered wood. The only color in the green meadow was the brilliant yellow of the sunflowers which grew along the side of the road.

"This must be where Rebecca lives," Nan said out loud to Little Red. In a moment, she thought, she would turn around, but she was curious. She decided to ride a little way into the meadow first. Slowly she rode along the road by the sunflowers, and beyond them, she could see a garden, with neatly weeded rows of vegetables.

Just when she had decided to turn around, a woman stood up in the middle of the vegetable garden. Little Red moved restlessly to one side, and Nan leaned over to quiet him. The woman was dressed in a brown color that blended into the background, so that Nan hadn't seen her until she moved. It must be Mrs. Snow, Nan thought. She had been weeding around the lettuce plants, and now she was standing by the sunflowers, with a bunch of weeds still in her hands.

"You're Nan Coburn, aren't you?" the woman said. "I've seen you with that pony when I've been downtown. Not that I get down very often. And Rebecca's always full of stories about you when she comes home from school. She'll be so glad you came to see her. She's down by the house tending her rabbits now. I mustn't keep you talking here. You'll be wanting to get on and play with her. Only none of us here sees people as much as we'd like, and when someone does come, we just can't stop talking."

"Oh, that's all right," Nan said. She didn't want to play with Rebecca. She wanted to keep on riding, but she couldn't very well turn back now. She could see that Mrs. Snow would be hurt. Nan didn't know what else to say, so she smiled and nodded and rode on toward the house.

Beside the house, Rebecca was kneeling by a row of wire cages. When she heard the pony come into the yard, she stood up and looked at Nan, her eyes big with surprise. For a moment, neither girl said anything.

Then Nan broke the silence. "Hello, Rebecca," she said.

Then Rebecca smiled. "You—you came to see me?" she asked.

Nan started to explain that it had just been by chance that she had taken the road through the woods that had brought her to Rebecca's house, but then she stopped. Instead she said, "Yes. Yes, I thought you might like to ride on Little Red."

"I would," Rebecca agreed. "And you can see my rabbits, if you want to. I've got some baby ones too."

"Have you ever ridden before?" Nan asked.

"Not on a pony," Rebecca answered. "Only on the work horse. I used to ride Shad a lot before we sold him. Before Daddy got hurt."

Nan wanted to ask what had happened to her father, but something held her back. Instead she said gruffly, "Well, you can ride if you want to."

She noticed how easily Rebecca settled into the saddle, and how quickly Little Red responded to her touch. "You handle him all right," Nan said. "He seems to feel comfortable with you."

Rebecca nodded, as thought this didn't surprise her. "Dad says I've got a way with animals," she said.

When Rebecca had ridden down to the garden to show the pony to her mother, Nan sat down on the edge of the porch to wait. Then from the open window in back of her, she heard a voice. "So you're Nan, are you?" the voice said. Nan turned around. Here, people always seemed to be in unexpected places. A man was leaning on the sill of the open window, and when Nan went closer she discovered that he was sitting in a brown wicker wheel chair and behind him was a little dog. She must have stared at the chair, for the man smiled. "This thing," he said. "It's the way I get around now. Since I fell in the hay loft, my legs don't work any more, and I push myself around in this. My, but that's a fine pony you've got."

He smiled. "And it's nice of you to come and see my Becky. Shut in the way we are, she doesn't get to play with children much." Then he wheeled himself off into the darkness inside the house. "Come on, Biscuit," he said and the dog followed along after the chair.

When Rebecca came back with Little Red she was letting him trot. "That was fun," she said to Nan.

"You can ride some more," Nan offered.

"I'll let him rest now," Rebecca said, "and we can look at the rabbits. If you want to, that is."

Rebecca reached into the back of one cage and brought out a small white bunny. She put it gently in Nan's hands. The bunny shivered and wrinkled his nose and then settled down. His fur was thick and white, and his eyes were a pure translucent pink. "Oh, he's lovely," Nan cried. Then she realized that she was having a very

good time and that she liked Rebecca. "This is fun," she said. "I like this, the bunny and everything. Jean never likes to do anything with animals."

Rebecca's face turned sad. "She's your best friend, isn't she?" she said to Nan.

"Well, she's . . ." Nan began and then stopped. It was very hard to say just what Jean was. "Sometimes she is, but other times she doesn't want to play at all, or she gets cross if I don't play just the games she likes."

"I know," Rebecca agreed. "She teases people an awful lot. And she bit you, the day she fell off the pony. And it really wasn't your fault at all."

Then before she remembered that she was never going to tell anyone, Nan found herself telling Rebecca the story about the prize cup that really didn't belong to Jean at all. Almost before she had finished, she began to have a guilty feeling that she had done something wrong. She had been unfair to Jean. She looked at Rebecca crossly as though it had been somehow her fault that she had told. And she was ready to defend Jean, if Rebecca said anything unkind.

But Rebecca didn't seem to notice. She held a piece of clover under the bunny's nose and sighed, "Poor Jean." Then she hopped up. "I'll race you down to the spring house for a drink of water." They were both off in an instant, running at top speed down the dusty road.

That evening, Nan sat on the porch at home watching the barn swallows sweep in a lazy chittering circle over the farm. She was thinking about Rebecca, her new friend, and Jean, her old friend. They were very different, she decided, and they didn't like the same things at all. Jean was fun to be with, sometimes, and she made life seem exciting and full of laughter. And Rebecca was fun in a different, quieter way. It was fun to talk about animals with her, and she seemed to understand about people, and how they get hurt inside. She seemed to know that Jean hadn't meant to do a bad thing when she bragged about the riding prize. Nan thought she would like to play with Rebecca again soon. Her family didn't seem sad and strange, the way she had thought they would. Maybe she would ride out there again tomorrow. The only trouble was that Jean never liked it when Nan played with other girls, and when Jean got angry about something, sometimes she wouldn't play with Nan for a long, long time. Nan sighed. Then she got up and went into the house. She found her mother sitting alone in the living room. Nan leaned on the arm of her mother's chair.

"I made a new friend today," she said.

Mrs. Coburn stopped writing in her diary and put her arm around Nan. "That's nice," she said. "Who is it?"

"It's Rebecca Snow," Nan answered. "And it's

strange. At first I didn't really want to play with her. I just got there by mistake. But when we played together, it was fun. It was . . ." Nan searched in her mind for a way to tell her mother about Rebecca. "Playing with her was like picking violets," she said suddenly.

Mrs. Coburn smiled and tightened her arm around Nan. "Yes," she said, "I know what you mean. She's shy, and you have to be gentle with her."

Nan nodded. "And playing with Jean is like picking roses," she went on.

"Pretty, but sort of prickly?" her mother asked and they both laughed.

"I thought you liked Jean," Nan said. "You're always saying I should play with her, and it's my fault if she cries and goes home."

Mrs. Coburn reached up and pushed the hair back from Nan's forehead. "I'd like you to play with both Jean and Rebecca," she said. "There are good things about them both—and some difficult ones too."

Nan leaned back against her mother's shoulder and thought how nice it was when her mother understood exactly how she felt.

8

Jumping

There were times when Nan's mother understood how she felt about things, but there were other times when she didn't seem to understand at all. In the summer, one of Nan's chores was to help keep the garden weeded. Mrs. Coburn couldn't understand why Nan got tired of the job. When the plants first started to poke through the ground, Nan went to the garden nearly every day to see what was happening. She liked the garden then because it was exciting and full of surprises.

One day there would be nothing but brown earth between the sticks that marked the ends of the rows. The next day there would be a tiny crack running along the row, with a tip of green showing here and there. And a day or two later, there would be a thin green line, with the shapes of the different leaves already visible, so that if you looked closely, you could see the flat spade shape that would be radish leaves or the feathery spike of carrots.

But now everything was well up out of the ground and the weeds were growing too. It was not very interesting to pull weeds, and Nan usually forgot about the garden until her mother reminded her. "You'd better do a row of carrots this morning," Mrs. Coburn had said after breakfast, and now Nan was in the garden, grubbing out weeds. The sun was warm on her back and she made up a soft tuneless carrot song, as she worked her way along the row.

At first when she heard the swishing sound in the grass beyond the garden, she thought it must be the cat, and she didn't look up. Then the noise seemed too loud for a cat, but when she stood up to look, she could only see the top of the grass waving, as though some large animal was making its way toward her. She picked up a clod of dirt and threw it into the grass.

"Ow!" said a voice and then Bob Connor stood up, smiling sheepishly. "I thought I was going to surprise you," he said, "but you surprised me instead."

He came out of the field and into the garden. "Want to go riding?" he asked. "I've been teaching my pony to jump and it's a lot of fun. Come on home with me, and you can try it with Little Red too."

"Okay," Nan said. "I'd like to. But I can't come for a while yet. I've got to finish weeding the carrots first."

"I'll help," Bob offered. "It won't take long that way."

Bob started at the far end of the row and in a few

minutes, when Nan looked up, she found that Bob had already finished more than half the row. In another minute, Bob had reached the spot where she was working.

Nan stood up. "You work a lot faster than I do," she said.

Bob brushed the dirt off his hands. "No sense in wasting time with a lot of weeds," he said.

Nan looked down at the place where he had worked and it was true that the weeds were all gone, but in some places, the row of carrots looked very thin and patchy. "Oh, Bob," Nan cried, "you pulled a lot of the carrots too."

"Did I?" Bob asked in surprise.

Nan poked at a pile of weeds with her toe. "Look, here's a whole handful of carrots."

"Well, don't worry," Bob said. "We'll just stick them back in the ground again." He scooped some dirt out, pushed the carrots into the hole and smoothed the dirt around them again.

"I don't think they'll grow like that," Nan said doubtfully.

"Well, let's put them back in and see. They might grow, and it won't do any harm to try."

"All right, but let's hurry," Nan grumbled. "It's getting hot out here in the sun."

By the time they had finished with the carrots and then caught Little Red and put the saddle on him, they were hotter than ever. Together they rode along the street to Bob's house and they were glad when they reached the cool shade in the backyard. There, Bob showed Nan how he had balanced a round pole across the top of two nail kegs.

"See, it rolls off easily enough so if a pony hits it when he's jumping, it won't trip him up. And that's about the right height, once they get the idea. Now watch."

Bob took his pony to the end of the yard and then cantered back toward the kegs. Just as they reached the bar, the pony paused and then with a spring went up and over the jump.

"That looks easy," Nan said.

"We've been practicing for two or three days," Bob said. "At first he wouldn't jump; he'd turn just at the last minute and go around the barrels instead. You try it with Little Red now."

Nan sent Little Red cantering toward the bar, but when he had almost reached it, he swerved sideways and went around the keg instead of jumping.

"See, what did I tell you?" Bob shouted. "That's just what my pony did."

Nan turned Little Red and let him smell of the bar. Then she took him back and tried again. This time, she held him straight on toward the bar, but when he reached it, he dug in his feet and balked.

"Maybe we'll have to put the bar down lower until he gets used to the idea," Bob said. "I had to do that at first."

Nan scowled at him. "Why didn't you tell me that?" she said crossly. "Why did you let me keep trying with this high thing?"

"Because I wanted to see if he'd act the same way," Bob explained. "You can't tell—he might have jumped the first time."

Nan nodded in agreement, but secretly she wished that Little Red had jumped the first time and surprised Bob.

Bob pulled the kegs away and set two flat stones in their place. Then he laid the bar across the stones, not more than a few inches off the ground. "There, try that," he said.

Nan brought Little Red up to the low bar and just when she thought he was going to refuse to go over even that, he gave a little spring and jumped. And even in that low jump, Nan could feel the power and surge of the pony under her.

"That's fun," she called.

"Try it a few more times," Bob advised. "Then I'll put the bar back on the barrels, so he really has to jump."

Nan took Little Red over the low hurdle until he jumped smoothly and easily.

"All right, now we'll try the kegs," Bob said.

Nan showed Little Red the high bar on the kegs and then she turned him and cantered toward the bar. For a moment he paused and Nan thought he wasn't going to try. Then he gave a spring that almost threw her off, and he went over the bar. He touched it with his hind feet and sent it clattering down behind them, but he had jumped. The next time around, he went over without touching the bar at all, and it felt to Nan as though they were flying when they went up and over the jump.

That afternoon, Nan made a jump for Little Red and put him back and forth over it, until he could jump every

time as smoothly as though he was one of the swallows that swooped over the roof of the barn. Frequently they stopped to rest, and Nan stroked the pony's nose. Together she and Little Red had learned something new, and she was glad.

Once when they were resting, Nan noticed that the white puffy clouds that had been in the sky earlier had turned into rolling gray thunderheads that covered almost the whole sky. She began to hear the distant roll of thunder. It seemed hotter than ever, even though the sun had disappeared. She got on Little Red and sent him trotting out of the yard toward the pasture. It was almost milking time, and her father would want to get the cows in earlier than usual, if it was going to rain.

Nan urged Little Red up the stony lane to the pasture. The air was still and heavy now, and Nan knew that the rain would come before very long. She got off at the pasture bars, and above her, she could see the cows huddled together under her grandfather's willow tree. They knew it was going to rain too. Nan hurried with the bars, but when she got to the lowest one, she realized that it was no higher than the bar Little Red had been jumping. She decided she would give him one last jump for the day and then take down the bar for the cows. Quickly she got on the pony and took him a few paces down the lane. Then she turned and sent him toward the bar.

As they came close, she saw that the bar looked higher than it had, because they were going uphill. Perhaps he will balk again, she thought, and she set herself in the saddle so that she wouldn't be thrown if he did. But he was not going to balk; she could feel him getting ready to jump, and they they were up and almost over. Next there was a crack and a clatter and Nan was pitched forward onto the ground and Little Red was down beside her and scrambling for his footing.

It happened so fast that Nan didn't have time to be frightened. Instinctively she rolled away from Little Red, and for a moment after that the world seemed to go black around her. Then she heard Little Red nicker softly, but the sound seemed far away. She sat up, and she was surprised to find Little Red standing over her. He nickered again and nuzzled her shoulder. He's asking me if I'm all right, she thought. Slowly, she stood up. Her shoulder ached when she moved her arm and one leg was sore, but nothing seemed to be broken. She patted Little Red. "Okay, boy," she said. "I'm all right."

The lower bar was cracked where Little Red's hoof had caught on it, and it sagged in the middle. Nan dragged it out of the way and thought, we'll have to get a new bar. She didn't want to think about what had happened just yet, and she was glad that she had to get the cows home quickly ahead of the storm.

By the time she had moved the bar, the cows had crowded in a semi-circle around her, and she had started them down the lane, when a sudden gust of wind pulled at the treetops. In a minute, the trees were whipping in the wind, so that they almost seemed to turn inside out. Nan could see the sheets of rain coming closer along the hillside. She hurried the cows as much as she could, but the rain caught them before she got them into the barnyard. The wind was so sharp and the drops of rain so big that they stung her bare arms, and she raced Little Red through the yard and right into the horse barn, without getting off.

When she had rubbed Little Red down and put him in his stall, Nan looked at him thoughtfully. She remembered the first time he had thrown her in the mud and how she had not wanted to ride him again, and her father had made her. That time she had been more frightened than hurt. And she remembered the time, not very long ago, when Little Red had kicked her, because she hadn't handled him properly, and she had had a terrible guilty feeling until she had told her family about it. This time, she realized, she had put Little Red over a jump that he wasn't ready to try. But afterwards, nobody had to tell her to get back on and ride him home. Nobody had to tell her what she had done wrong, and she didn't feel guilty, because she knew that she had learned something. She hadn't just learned how to use a whip or how high a jump to put a pony over. She had learned that she herself had to be responsible for what happened to herself and Little Red.

9

The Pony Cart

During the rest of the summer, Nan was so busy that the time flew by. Some days she helped her father with the haying. Sometimes she played with Jean or went riding with Bob. A few times, she rode out to visit Rebecca. Almost before she knew it, it was time for school to start, and although she liked the summer, when she could ride Little Red whenever she wanted, she was glad now to go back to school.

But just a few days after school opened, Nan came down with the mumps. At first she was quite sick and she didn't mind missing school. Then one day, she woke up feeling much better. She felt too good to stay inside the house any longer, but the doctor had said she couldn't go back to school until every bit of the swelling was gone, because she might expose somebody else to the mumps. Grownups were so fussy, Nan thought.

She went out and sat on the edge of the porch, and for a while she was satisfied. It was nice, just to sit in the sun and feel it warm on her, almost like a bath in air. But then she got tired of just sitting, and she got up and started to jump down the steps with both feet together. She was surprised to find that that made her mumps hurt, so she stopped jumping and walked down. She wished she could ride Little Red, but she knew they wouldn't let her, and anyway, maybe that would hurt too.

Then Nan had an idea. She would go upstairs in the carriage house and look around. She hadn't been up there for a long time. It was dusty and full of spiders, she knew, but she couldn't remember exactly what was up there. It would be fun to explore.

She climbed up the carriage house stairs, and when she reached the top she drew in her breath. It was like a fairyland. The sun shining through the window at the end of the shed struck through dozens of spider webs and the room looked as though it was decorated for a party. And along each side of the shed there were old sleighs and wagons, as though the guests had driven right in, she thought.

Nan went over to the nearest sleigh and brushed some of the dust from the seat. Under the dust, the seat was black leather, with deep creases and black leather buttons where the lines crossed. Quickly she brushed off more dust and got in. The front of the sleigh curved gracefully, and when she blew the dust off, she could see a design painted on it in neat gold lines.

Nan sat in the sleigh and imagined how it would be to drive Little Red over snowy fields. He would have to have a little harness, and a string of bells across his back. If the roads weren't too icy, she might even be able to drive up to see Rebecca. Rebecca would be so pleased. Then with a pang of loyalty, Nan remembered Jean. She would take Jean for a ride too, if Jean would go. Even Jean shouldn't be frightened of riding in a sleigh.

She began to hum "Jingle Bells" and she could almost hear the jog-jog of Little Red's feet and the jingle-jingle of his bells. I could really do it, she thought. If her father would help her get the sleigh down and then fix an old harness so that it was small enough. But it would be a long time before there was any snow, and it was such a nice idea, she wanted to drive Little Red right now.

She got out of the sleigh and looked at the wagons, but they were all too big and they were not pretty like the sleigh. Then Nan looked up, and there she saw a two-wheeled box cart. It had been pulled up and hung from the rafters by ropes, and it looked just right for Little Red. When she climbed up on the back of a wagon, she could just reach the bottom of the wheels. She could hardly wait to get the cart down, but she would have to find someone to help her. She jumped down from the back of the wagon and hurried off to look for her father.

"My goodness, just look at you!" her mother exclaimed, when Nan came into the kitchen. "You are as black as a boot. Where in the world have you been to get so dirty?"

"Up in the carriage house," Nan explained. "Where's Dad? I've got to tell him something."

"He'll be coming in to eat any minute now. And you just get cleaned up and ready for dinner yourself."

"But I have to tell you, I found the most wonderful thing," Nan began.

Her mother smiled. "All right, Nan, after you get washed up, you can tell me," she said.

As soon as they were all at the table, Nan told about finding the little cart. When she had finished, her grandfather had a faraway smile on his face.

"By golly," he said, "that brings back memories. That cart was the one I gave your grandmother when we were first married. And a little driving mare named Nellie. Oh, how that mare could step along."

"Do you think we could get the cart down and I could drive Little Red in it?" Nan asked.

"I don't see any reason why not," her grandfather said. "I don't know why I didn't think of that before now. It won't be too heavy. Might be a little long in the shafts, but I guess we can fix that."

"And we could take an old harness and cut it down," Nan suggested.

"Nellie's harness must be up there somewhere. We ought to be able to shorten the straps so it would fit. She wasn't so big herself."

"Oh, can we do it today?" Nan asked.

Later, up in the carriage house, she skipped excitedly from place to place while she watched her father and grandfather loosen the ropes and lower the little cart to the floor. Then they rolled it to the big window at the end of the shed and carefully, with a pulley, they swung it out of the window and lowered it to the ground.

"We'll need some old rags, Pumpkin Face," her father said.

Her father got a pail of water, while her grandfather went back to the carriage house to hunt for the harness.

Nan brought some strips of cloth torn from an old pillowcase and helped her father. First they brushed off as much dust as they could, and then Mr. Coburn sloshed water over the wagon and Nan rubbed off the dirt. She could see the deep blue color, now, and the gold lines of the trim. They worked on the wagon for some time and then her father said, "That's about the best we can do, I guess. It looks pretty good. Now when we get the harness fixed, you can try it out."

That night her grandfather cleaned the harness with saddle soap and shortened the straps as much as he could. "There," he said. "Tomorrow we can see how Little Red likes pulling a cart."

The next morning Nan could hardly wait until her grandfather had finished his chores at the barn and was ready to help her with Little Red. Nan's mumps were gone, but today she was glad that she couldn't go to school. She wanted to spend the whole day with Little Red and the new cart. At first Little Red didn't like the cart, and when they tried to back him into it, he wouldn't move. Her grandfather held the shafts up and Nan tried to make him back into them. Then Nan held the shafts and her grandfather tried to make Little Red move. Then her grandfather said, "Well, if we can't back him into the shafts, we'll try moving the cart up to him."

Nan held the pony and her grandfather moved the cart up until the shafts were in position on either side of him. They hitched the tugs and back straps in place, and Nan's grandfather took the reins. "Now climb in," he said. Then he handed the reins to Nan and climbed in beside her. He made a clicking noise with his tongue, and Little Red started off with short, jerky steps and tried to look around to see what was following him. But after a few trips around the yard, he began to walk smoothly.

Her grandfather leaned back on the seat beside Nan and sighed. "This beats an automobile any day," he said.

On Saturday morning, Nan hitched Little Red to the cart and started off down the road. It had rained in the night, and there was a damp smell of wet leaves in the air. The trees were bare, and the grass beside the road had turned brown. But now the sun was coming out warm, and the fog was rising up from the river, and Nan was glad to be out again. It was two weeks since she had been allowed to leave her own yard, and she felt excited with her freedom.

She had called Jean on the phone before she left home, and when she reached her house, Jean was waiting on the porch for her.

Jean nodded approvingly. "That's a nifty cart," she said.

Nan smiled. She was glad that Jean was in a good mood. "Hop in," she said, and Jean did.

They drove slowly through the village, and Jean sat up very straight and waved to all the people they met. "We can pretend this is the queen's chariot," Jean said. "And you are the footman."

"I'd better be the coachman," Nan replied. "Somebody has to drive."

"All right," Jean agreed. "You can be the coachman and the footman."

When they reached the end of the village and Nan turned off on a dirt road, Jean objected. "Can't we just ride back and forth through the town?" she asked.

"The asphalt is too hard on Little Red's feet," Nan explained.

"Oh, well," Jean sighed. "But let's not go too far."

Nan sent the pony into a trot and the wheels whirred through the damp sand and the spokes blurred together so that the wheel looked solid.

"Isn't this fun?" Nan asked. "Don't you like it?"

"It's better than riding," Jean acknowledged. Then she put her hand up to shield her eyes from the sun. "I wonder who that is?"

Far up the road ahead of them, Nan could see someone walking. As they came closer, Nan realized that the figure was Rebecca, but she did not say anything. She wanted to stop and give Rebecca a ride, but she wasn't sure that Jean would like it. Jean was being so nice today, perhaps it would be all right. Perhaps they could all three be friends. When they came even with Rebecca, Nan saw that she was carrying a bag of groceries. Nan waved and then pulled Little Red down to a walk.

"Let's give her a ride home," Nan said.

"O—oo," Jean groaned.

Nan stopped Little Red and waited for Rebecca to catch up to them. "It won't hurt you," she whispered to Jean. "Really, she's nice when you get to know her." Jean didn't say anything, but she made a face at Nan. Then Nan turned and called to Rebecca. "Come on, we'll give you a ride."

Rebecca was walking with her head down and her

arms clasped around a heavy brown paper bag. "I don't mind walking really," she mumbled. "And it would be crowding you."

"That's all right," Nan assured her. She hopped out of the wagon and motioned for Jean to make room for Rebecca on the seat beside her. Rebecca got in and set the groceries at her feet. At the last moment, Jean made a great deal of noise moving her feet out of the way, as though the bag might be filled with snakes.

"That's awfully heavy for you," Nan said.

Rebecca ducked her head and said again, "I don't mind really."

For a while they rode along in silence and Nan tried to think of something to say. She wished Jean would say something bright and funny, but she didn't.

Finally Nan said, "Do you have any new animals?"

Rebecca smiled and lifted her head a little. "No," she said, "but I've taught Biscuit to roll over."

"How did you do that?" Nan asked.

"With a biscuit," Rebecca said, and they both laughed. "I'd get him to lie down and then hold a biscuit close to his nose, and I'd roll his feet over for him and then give him the biscuit to eat. After a while he got the idea, and now he rolls over all by himself when I tell him to."

"It must have taken a lot of patience," Nan commented.

Rebecca nodded and then the silence settled down over the cart again. After a while, Jean leaned forward and looked at Rebecca. "That's a very pretty dress you have on," she said.

Rebecca looked at Jean out of the corner of her eye and then said, "Thank you."

"Sally Barglow used to have one just like it," Jean continued. "But I haven't seen her wear it lately."

Rebecca's face turned a deep red and she ducked her head even lower than usual.

"I guess this used to be Sally's dress," she mumbled. "It came in the Christmas box from the church."

Nan looked straight ahead at Little Red's ears and she was gripping the reins so hard that her hands hurt. Inside, she was furious with Jean but she couldn't think of anything to say that wouldn't make Rebecca feel worse than she did already.

Then suddenly she felt Rebecca move beside her and she looked around. Rebecca's face was still red, but she was holding her head up now. "I know we're poor," she said, "and it's nothing to be ashamed of, but I can't help it—being ashamed. But you've got nothing to be so proud of, either, Jean Ross. My father cut some wood for your father the winter before he was hurt, and he's never been paid for it. Perhaps if your father paid his bills, I wouldn't have to wear hand-me-downs all the time."

Again there was silence. This time Jean's face was red,

and she was staring off into space. At last she spoke. "I didn't know that about the money," she said in a quiet voice. "I'm sorry. And I'm sorry I said that about your dress too."

The two girls looked at each other for a moment. Then Rebecca smiled and said, "That's all right. I'm sorry for what I said too. It isn't your fault."

When they reached the Snow farm, Nan got out and helped Rebecca with the bag of groceries. She was surprised to see Jean getting out too. Jean came around the cart and stood by Rebecca. "Would you show us Biscuit's new trick?" she asked.

When they had watched Biscuit perform, Jean and Nan got back in the cart, waved good-bye to Rebecca and started back toward town. For a while neither of them said anything. Then Jean began to cry softly, and for the second time that day, Nan didn't know what to say. Instead of saying anything, she found a clean handkerchief in her pocket and quietly slipped it into Jean's hand.

When Jean had stopped crying and wiped her eyes, she looked at Nan and said, "It's true, you know. I've heard people talking to my father about money, and they're angry sometimes. And my mother and my father talk about it too, and my mother says we must pay the bills and not be so extravagant, and my father just laughs and says, 'Why worry? We're having fun!' And it makes me feel awful. I wish I was poor like Rebecca and didn't have things. I keep thinking everybody must know about it. And I say mean things to people because I feel mean inside."

Nan put her arm on Jean's shoulder. "It's not your fault," she said. She felt closer to Jean than she ever had before. And now she thought she would understand when Jean was moody and cross sometimes.

"You'd better tend to the driving," Jean said, "or we'll end up in the ditch."

"Oh, Little Red wouldn't do that," Nan said, but she put both hands back on the reins, and Jean began to chatter on about Bob Connor's new Indian pony, and Nan knew that she didn't want to talk about her family any more.

When she got home, Nan had taken care of Little Red and was putting the cart into the shed, when her grandfather came out of the house.

"Well, have you been showing off your wagon and giving rides to half the town?" he teased.

"I only took two people for a ride," Nan said, "Jean and Rebecca."

"Both at the same time?" her grandfather asked.

Nan nodded.

"I shouldn't think your cart was big enough for you to give two people a ride at once," he said.

Nan began to laugh. "For a while I didn't think any

cart would be big enough for those two to ride in to-gether," she said.

Then she told her grandfather what had happened. When she finished, her grandfather looked thoughtful. Then he clapped her on the shoulder.

"You know," he said, "most people in this world have got problems of one sort or another. Just like Jean and Rebecca. If you remember that, you've gone a long way toward understanding why they act the way they do. It's part of growing up to understand that."

10

Too Big for Little Red

Nan was glad that her grandfather thought she was
growing up. But it wasn't just in knowing about people
that she was growing. That winter she began to grow
tall, and mostly she was glad about that too.

For two years she hadn't grown much at all, but now
it seemed as if she would never stop growing. At school
her knees bumped against the bottom of her desk. And
at home, her mother had let down the hems on all her
skirts, saying, half grumbling at the work, half proud
of such a big daughter, that she was growing like a weed.
Mrs. Coburn even let her have her hair cut, as though
she was grown up now and could decide for herself.

When the school glee club sang in assembly, Nan
liked standing in the back row with the older children.
She liked the new wool skirts her mother had made for

her when the old ones couldn't be let down any more. And she liked the stubby feeling of her hair, cut short just below her ears; she liked not having to stand still while her mother combed and braided every morning, and only a very little, she missed the swing and bob of her pigtails. But there was one thing she didn't like at all about growing. She was getting too big for Little Red.

In the barn, she could lean on Little Red without raising her arms. She could swing her leg over his back and get on without much of a jump. And when she was on, her feet dangled nearly to the ground. The stirrup straps had been let out as far as they would go and they still weren't long enough for her. And when she got on Little Red, he grunted and looked around as though he was surprised to find anyone so heavy on his back.

In April, the weather turned warm, and the snow melted and ran off in spring rivulets down the road. Then in a few days, the worst of the mud dried up, and there was a tinge of green showing in the grass.

"It's time you gave that pony a little exercise," Mr. Coburn said to Nan.

Nan looked thoughtful. "I might be too big for him," she said. "Too heavy for him, I mean. It might hurt him."

"No," her father scoffed. "You won't hurt him. He's a tough little scamp. He can carry a bigger load than you."

"Maybe I could just drive him in the cart."

"He'll be pretty lively with no more exercise than he's had all winter. You'd better ride him a few times before you try hitching him up to the cart."

Last year, when she had taken Little Red out for the first time in the spring, she had been a bit frightened, but very happy and excited too, as if she had a surprise package to open. But now she was not frightened or excited or happy. She just felt a sort of dull ache growing inside her and she wished very much that she could squeeze up and shrink so that she would be just the right size for Little Red again.

Nan looked at the pony saddle. She couldn't use the stirrups, and the saddle itself was uncomfortably small for her. She could ride Little Red bareback; she did that sometimes in the summer. But he was likely to shy and jump when he hadn't been exercised for a long time. She wasn't certain she could stay on without a saddle, even if she was big. Then she had an idea. Her father had an old Army saddle in the harness room. Sometimes he used it on one of the work horses if he needed to go far up into the hills to look for a stray cow. That would be big enough for her and she could use it on Little Red, she thought, if she could shorten the cinch straps from big horse size down to pony size.

The leather of the cinch straps was old and stiff and

it took Nan a long time to tighten up both sides. Little Red stood patiently, with his head turned to watch her. At last she got both straps shortened and then she tightened up the cinch. But when she had pulled it up as tight as it would go, it still flapped loosely under the pony's belly. Suddenly Nan stood back and looked at Little Red and began to laugh. The huge lump of the horse saddle on his back made him look like a big dog pretending to be a pony. Then when she had finished laughing, Nan had another idea. She took the short cinch from the pony saddle and strapped it in place of the horse saddle cinch. Then the saddle was held in place, tight and secure. Next she adjusted the stirrups, and when they were comfortable, she took Little Red out into the yard. She was beginning to feel excited and happy after all.

She rode Little Red through the yard and into the field. She pushed him into a trot along the wagon road and then into a canter. At the plank bridge across the brook, he suddenly braced both feet and stopped. Sometimes Nan had been thrown over his head when he stopped like that, but now she caught herself easily and settled back in the saddle. Little Red sniffed the air with both nostrils wide. He looked at the bridge as though he had never seen it before. Nan pressed her knees into his sides and touched him on the flank with the ends of the reins. Slowly he moved one foot forward onto the bridge, and then waited uncertainly. Nan touched him again and he scrambled across the bridge in two jumps, breathing hard, and then settled down into a trot. Nan turned him back to the bridge and again he stopped and then hurried across. She rode him back and forth over the bridge until he crossed it willingly, even at a trot.

She patted the pony's neck. "Good Little Red," she said.

She rode Little Red to the far end of the field and turned him. Then she dug both knees into his sides and yelled, "Go!" Little Red jumped forward and sped across the field, and to Nan it felt as though they were flying. Nan leaned low over Little Red's neck. With his mane blowing in her face and the ground flying by under his feet, she felt like laughing for the sheer joy of it. With a clatter of hooves they went over the bridge and down into the yard, where she pulled him up in front of the house.

She got off and tightened the saddle again. Then she rode Little Red out of the yard and turned him down the road toward the village. Her grandfather might be playing checkers with the men at the feed store, and she wanted to show him how she had fixed the saddle and tell him how well Little Red was behaving this year. When she reached the feed store there were several men lounging on the steps, but she didn't see her grandfather.

She stopped the pony. "Has my grandfather been around?" she asked.

The men looked up and one of them nodded. "He was here a while ago. I think he went over to the bank," the man said.

"Say," said another man, "aren't you getting pretty big for that pony?"

Nan ducked her head. "Sort of," she said. She turned Little Red and started to ride away.

"Yeah," one of the men called after her, "why don't you get off and carry the pony?"

The place rocked with laughter, and Nan could feel her face and the back of her neck getting red. She wished she could hide some place, or be so small no one could see her. It seemed to take a long time to get around the corner out of sight of the men, and all the time she could hear them chuckling. When they were out of sight, she put Little Red into a trot and went home and put him in his stall. She took off his saddle and changed the saddle cinches back again. She knew now she would never want to ride Little Red again. She thought how well he had behaved when she made him cross the bridge and how he had run the length of the field, flying like the wind. But she didn't want to ride him any more. There was no question about it; she was too big for Little Red.

Nan put her face down against Little Red's neck and her tears rolled into the thick black hair of his mane. She wasn't crying now because she had been teased and had

felt first ridiculous and then angry. She was crying because she knew that she really had outgrown Little Red.
She could drive him in the cart, but that wasn't the
same. She could ride him in the pasture where no one
would see. Perhaps she could even make herself ride him
on the street again, not caring if someone teased. But
that wouldn't change the fact that she was growing up
and that soon her feet would really reach the ground
when she tried to ride Little Red. She was crying because
things changed and she wanted them always to stay the
same.

She gave Little Red a hug around the neck and he
nibbled her elbow and then nickered as she walked
away.

At the supper table that night, her grandfather cleared
his throat and looked around the table. Then he looked
straight at Nan and said, "Henry Connor was telling
me some of the boys were teasing you over at the feed
store this afternoon."

Nan looked down at her plate and nodded.

"You don't want to let them bother you," her father
said, and Nan knew from the way he said it that her
grandfather had told him about what the men had said.

"I can't help it. I *am* too big," she said.

"Oh, squizzle!" Mrs. Coburn said. That was what
she said when she didn't agree with Nan and wanted to

make her forget something and laugh. But she couldn't laugh tonight. She just kept looking at her plate and tried not to cry.

"I see you were using the big saddle," Mr. Coburn commented.

Nan nodded, but the tears were still too close for her to try to talk.

"Well, maybe we ought to get you a big horse to go with the saddle," he said.

For a moment Nan didn't move. A horse—if she had a horse she could ride, and nobody would say she was too big, or make jokes about her.

"I hear they've got a Morgan mare up at Graham's they want to sell," her grandfather said, as though he had been thinking of buying a horse all along.

"That's a real pretty little roan mare they've got," Mr. Coburn agreed. "She's broken to saddle, and she'll drive in harness too."

"It would be kind of handy to have an extra horse to use on the rake during haying season," her grandfather agreed.

Nan looked up then and her father and grandfather were both smiling. Her mother was smiling too. Then Nan knew that they had planned it all ahead of time. They were going to get her a horse. They must have been talking about it even before today.

"If you hurry and clean up your plate, we might

drive over after supper and take a look at her," Mr. Coburn said.

Nan hadn't felt like eating before, but now she felt hungry again. When she had finished eating, she helped clear the table, and then they all got in the car, without even bothering to do the dishes, so that they could get to the Graham's farm while it was still light.

When they got there, Mr. Graham was waiting for them. He led the mare out of the barn, and Nan thought it was the most beautiful animal she had ever seen. She was a light red-roan color, and she stood almost as high as a work horse. Her body and legs were sturdy but not heavy. She stood easily, and her eyes shone brightly and intelligently, but without the wicked twinkle that Little Red's sometimes had.

"Want to try riding her?" Mr. Graham asked.

"Oh, yes, please," Nan said.

Mr. Graham put on a saddle and slipped a bridle over the mare's head. Nan went over to get on, but the bottom of the stirrup was almost as high as Little Red's back, and no matter how much she tried, she couldn't lift her foot high enough.

"I'll give you a hand up," Mr. Graham said. He held his cupped hand for Nan to step into and then gave her a boost into the saddle. "You'll need a mounting block, if you are going to get on by yourself."

At first Nan felt very high up. When she fell off Little

Red, she didn't have very far to fall, but if she fell off now—well, it seemed a long way down to the ground. But then she remembered when she had first ridden Little Red, it had seemed that way too. She spoke to the mare, and the mare twitched her ears and started to move off.

"What's her name?" Nan called back to Mr. Graham.

"Plum," shouted Mr. Graham. "Because she is sort of plum colored."

Nan circled back around the group that stood watching.

"She's got a good eye," her grandfather said.

"Oh, she's all right," Mr. Graham agreed. "A good easy little mare. Take her on down in the field if you want to and let her out a bit," he told Nan.

"Be careful!" Mrs. Coburn called after her.

Then Nan turned the mare toward the field and increased the pressure of her knees. She leaned over and whispered, "Go, Plum!" Plum settled into a smooth trot. Nan held her at a trot once around the field. Then she spoke to her again, and Plum began to canter. But when she cantered, she rocked back and forth as though the legs on one side of her body were shorter than those on the other. At first Nan was almost thrown out of the saddle, but then she began to expect the lurching movement and rode to it. It was better then, but it still wasn't a comfortable gait. She spoke to Plum again, and she

dropped back into a trot, and they trotted up the drive
to the yard.

"She's got a lovely trot," Nan said. "But she canters
like a—like a—"

"Like a rocking chair with one rocker broken," put in
Mr. Graham. "You've put your finger on it, there, Nan.
But you can sit to that trot of hers and she'll keep it up
hour after hour and never get up a sweat. She'll take you
along faster with that trot than most horses will running."

"How about it, Nan?" Mr. Coburn asked. "Does that
canter bother you? Would you rather look around for a
horse that doesn't have a broken rocker?"

Nan thought for a minute. With Little Red, she had
loved going fast, running free and wild into the wind.
But Plum was different; instead of wildness and speed
and laughter, she had gentleness. Nothing could ever
take the place of Little Red, and perhaps it was better
to have a different kind of horse now.

"I like Plum," Nan said. "And the canter isn't so bad,
when you are used to it."

"I've seen her work in harness," Mr. Coburn said.
"She looks like a good even worker."

While the men talked about the price and when they
could get the mare, Nan stood next to Plum and ran her
fingers along the smooth red-roan neck. It was funny,
she thought, how the hair grew like that, with two colors
mixed together. And pretty, too. She'd never seen a roan

pony; maybe only horses were roan. Then she thought of Little Red and wondered what would happen to him. It wouldn't be much fun for him with nobody to ride him. And the barn would be crowded with the work horses and Plum and Little Red.

Mr. Graham came over and took the reins from her, and her father called for her to come and get in the car.

"Well, she's all yours, Nan," her grandfather said when they drove out of the yard. "Mr. Graham will bring her down in his truck tomorrow."

"I was wondering," Nan said. "Where will we put her? There isn't an extra stall."

"Why, she'll have the box stall—Little Red's stall," her father said.

"Then where will Little Red go?" Nan asked, with a sinking feeling.

Her father looked surprised. "Why, I thought you knew," he said. "We'll have to sell Little Red."

"Sell Little Red?" Nan said. For a minute she couldn't believe that her father meant it. How could he think she would let Little Red go? He was her pony, even if she was too big to ride him. "I wouldn't sell Little Red ever." But deep inside her, the sinking feeling grew worse and the whole world seemed strange and cold.

"We can't just keep him around," her father said. "It wouldn't be fair to him. He's a young pony yet; he needs exercise, and you said yourself you didn't want to ride him again. Besides we can't just keep feeding him and not be getting any good out of him. And if you're going to have that mare, we've got to have someplace to put her."

"Then I don't want Plum," she said, her voice near to tears. "I'll just keep Little Red and exercise him in the cart."

"Wait a minute, now," her grandfather said. "How does this sound to you? When I was talking to Henry Connor this afternoon, he told me he was looking for a pony for his little boy—Bob's brother. If we can make a deal with the Connors to take Little Red, would that satisfy you? You'd have Little Red right near by, so you could see him. He'd have a good home and plenty of exercise. And we'd have room in the barn for your new mare."

"How about that, Nan?" her father asked.

They had made up their minds, Nan knew. It was almost as if they had been planning this, even before she said she would never ride Little Red again. Maybe they had already arranged to sell Little Red to the Connor's. They all seemed to be against her. They would do what they wanted, anyway, whether she liked it or not. And now they wanted her to say she liked it their way too. She stuck out her lower lip and scowled.

"I don't want a horse. Not ever," she said.

"I'll tell you what," her grandfather said. "How would it be if we tried it for a couple of weeks? You have the Morgan, and the Connors have the pony?"

"And if I still don't like it that way, can I have Little Red back?"

Her grandfather hesitated for a moment. Then he slapped his cap across his knee and said, "Yes, by gravy, if that's what you want."

The next morning, Nan put the halter on Little Red and led him down the road to the Connor's. She was glad there weren't any men standing around in front of the feed store when she went by. Her father had told her to take the pony down, and she had said that she would, but in her heart she didn't really want to. In spite of her grandfather's promise, she had a feeling that once the change was made, it would be for good.

She thought about the good times she and Little Red had together; about how, even yesterday, before the men had laughed at her, she had ridden Little Red through the fields, and it had seemed as though there was nothing in the world but the spring green of the grass flowing under them, and the cool air rushing past, and the two of them almost flying. Suddenly she knew that she had to ride Little Red once more before she gave him up. She would take him out on a back road, where there would be no one to laugh at them.

She led Little Red through town and out into the

country on the road to Rebecca's house. She didn't have
a saddle, but that would be all right. She had ridden
bareback before. She didn't have a bridle either and that
worried her a little. But then she decided that that would
be all right too. She knotted the halter rope around his
neck. Then she threw her leg over his back and with a
little spring she was on. "Okay, Little Red," she whispered. Little Red started off at an easy trot and then, as
if he knew this was their last ride, he stretched out and
began to run with the long easy lope that Nan loved. She
bent over his neck and they flew on until the cool air
rushing into her face brought tears to her eyes. Then she
pulled on the halter rope and he settled back into a trot.

When they reached the turn to the Snow's farm, Little
Red turned in, from long habit, and Nan didn't try to
stop him. We might as well go see Rebecca, she thought.
She won't laugh because I'm too big. They found
Rebecca moving her rabbit hutches into the sun and
Nan jumped off and helped her carry them. When they
had finished, Rebecca patted Little Red. Then she
looked up at Nan in surprise.

"You're riding him just with a halter," she said.

Nan nodded. Then she told Rebecca about the men
who had laughed at her, and about the new mare, Plum,
and how she would have to let Little Red go to the
Connor's.

"I wish . . ." Rebecca began and then blushed.

Nan looked at her and in an instant she knew what Rebecca had been going to say. Rebecca was smaller than Nan; she was still the smallest girl in the class. She would be able to ride Little Red for a long time.

"That's it!" Nan shouted. "You're the one who ought to have Little Red."

Rebecca's eyes shone. "Oh, Nan, that would be . . . it would be the most wonderful thing that has ever happened to me." Then she shook her head and the light went out of her eyes. "But it wouldn't work," she said. "We couldn't afford to buy a pony. I couldn't even ask."

"Of course not, silly. Don't you see? You'd be keeping Little Red for me. And giving him exercise. I'd rather have you have him than anybody else. And we could go riding together, so I'd still see Little Red."

"That's all right for you, Nan. But your father and your grandfather—they won't see it that way. You can't just give ponies away like . . . like kittens."

"But I'm not giving him away," Nan argued. "You're keeping him for me and that's different."

"Maybe," Rebecca said, "but it won't look that way to your folks."

"All right. But will you keep him, if my folks say it's okay?"

"I'll have to ask my father too," Rebecca said. "But I guess it will be all right."

Nan gave a loud whoop and danced around the rabbit

hutches and back to Rebecca. "I'm going to leave him here now and walk home," she said. "It will be all right. You'll see." Rebecca shook her head doubtfully, but she took hold of Little Red's halter and held him when Nan ran down the road toward home.

When she had reached home and quickly washed some of the dust from her hands and face and then rushed in to take her place at the dinner table, Nan didn't feel quite so certain about being able to convince everybody that Little Red should go to Rebecca. It occurred to her that she hadn't behaved very well that morning. She had been told to take Little Red to the Connor's right after breakfast. Instead she had taken him to Rebecca's and left him there. While she was doing it, she hadn't thought about it. It had just seemed to happen, and each thing had followed the other. But now that she stopped to think about it, she was frightened. She wasn't sure how to start telling about it. Before she could think how to begin, her father put down his fork and leaned across the table toward her.

"Mr. Connor called up about a half hour ago—wanted to know if we'd changed our minds about the pony deal." He stopped and looked at Nan.

"What . . . what did you tell him?" she stammered.

"I told him I guessed you must have gotten lost between here and there."

"Well, I did—sort of," Nan said. Then she blurted out the whole story of how she had taken Little Red out in the country for a last ride and then how they had gone to Rebecca's house and how she had suddenly had a wonderful idea about giving Little Red to Rebecca. "Not giving, exactly, but letting her keep him for me."

"Hmph," said her grandfather.

"And Rebecca loves animals so," Nan hurried on. "She would take awfully good care of him. Really. And she—well, she ought to have a pony."

"I don't know that I can afford to set up in business to provide ponies for all the children that ought to have them," her grandfather said. "It seems a mite unprofitable."

"And what about Bob Connor's brother?" her father asked. "He wants a pony too, doesn't he? What have you got against him?"

"Oh, nothing," Nan said. "Only—if he doesn't get Little Red, his father will get him another pony. But if Rebecca doesn't get Little Red, she'll never have any pony."

Her grandfather leaned back in his chair and twiddled his thumbs. He looked at Nan thoughtfully and twiddled his thumbs some more. Then he said, "I don't know that your idea is too bad. Seems like in a few years Rebecca will get too big for Little Red too. And that pony will still have a lot of life in him. Maybe then we'll be able to find somebody else that really ought to have a pony. I guess in the meantime, we can afford to lend him to Rebecca for a little while. Course we'll have to get this settled with the Snows and let the Connors know and all that."

"Oh, thank you, Grandpa," Nan said, and she felt like crying because she was so pleased.

"Well, you've had a lot of fun with that pony since the time you worked so hard to get a hundred and ten in arithmetic. You've learned a lot about horses and maybe a little bit about arithmetic. But I don't think I'll ever make you into a horse trader."

"More of a horse giver," her father put in.

"Not that you haven't got some good points," her grandfather continued.

Nan ducked her head and she felt a warm glow from her grandfather's praise.

Then Mrs. Coburn began to laugh. "You men!" she said. "I think maybe Nan's the smartest horse trader in the family. She talked you into getting her a new mare yesterday, and today she's talked you into keeping Little Red. I should call that some pretty smart horse trading."

About the Author

Roberta Piper grew up in an old 19th century farmhouse in Vermont. She was graduated from the University of Vermont and received an M.A. at Columbia University where she met her husband Dan. The Pipers now live in Carbondale, Illinois with their sons, Andrew and Jonathan.

Mrs. Piper enjoys many activities, among them tennis, swimming, woodworking, and ceramics. However, she does not consider writing one of her hobbies. "For me, it is work—frequently very satisfying, but work." LITTLE RED is her first book for young readers.

About the Artist

Joan Berg was born in Chicago, Illinois. She studied art at Newcomb College of Tulane University in New Orleans and received her M.F.A. degree from the Yale University School of Art and Architecture.

As a free-lance artist and illustrator she has contributed to *Harper's, The Reporter,* and other magazines. Miss Berg's work has appeared in art shows and exhibitions in Chicago and New Orleans, and in 1962 she had her first one-man show in New York.